Christiana Flanigan

HIGH LIFE IN VERDOPOLIS

Charlotte Brontë's

HIGH LIFE
IN
VERDOPOLIS

A story from
the Glass Town Saga

presented with
facsimile illustrations from the manuscript
and drawings by Charlotte Brontë herself

INTRODUCED AND EDITED BY
CHRISTINE ALEXANDER

THE BRITISH LIBRARY
1995

© 1995 The British Library Board

First published 1995 by
The British Library
Great Russell Street
London WC1B 3DG

British Library Cataloguing in Publication Data
A cataloguing record for this publication is
available from The British Library

ISBN 0-7123-0408-8

Designed by John Mitchell
Typeset in Caslon 540 by
Nene Phototypesetters Ltd,
Northampton
Colour plates printed by
York House Graphics,
Hanwell, Middlesex
Printed in England by
St Edmundsbury Press,
Bury St Edmunds

For Rebecca & Roland

CONTENTS

INTRODUCTION

In her Preface to *The Professor*, Charlotte Brontë wrote that 'A first attempt it certainly was not as the pen which wrote it had been previously worn down a good deal in a practice of some years'. *High Life In Verdopolis* was part of this early 'practice', written in the 'wild weird writing' that Elizabeth Gaskell alluded to in 1857 when she published the first biography of Charlotte Brontë, who had died two years earlier. It is a romance, one of many fantastic tales woven around the imaginary African kingdom of Glass Town, and of central importance to the development of Charlotte's hero, the Duke of Zamorna.

The manuscript of *High Life In Verdopolis* was left in Brussels when Charlotte returned home to Haworth in January 1844, after two years at school there. It appears that she gave the manuscript, together with several other stories, to her revered teacher Constantin Heger, perhaps as an example of her more successful writing. Whatever the case, the owner undoubtedly treasured the gift as a souvenir of a famous novelist, since the manuscripts were handsomely bound in leather and embossed in gold lettering on the front cover: 'Manuscrits de Miss Charlotte Brontë (Currer Bell)'. Then, mysteriously, the little volume was found in a second hand bookstall in Brussels, and soon after, in 1892, offered to the British Museum for £25. There, in splendid anonymity, *High Life In Verdopolis* remained, unknown and unpublished until 1991. The present volume is the first occasion that this novelette has been published alone as an example of Charlotte Brontë's playful apprenticeship in literary composition.

The tale was composed when Charlotte was seventeen, at a time when she was immersed in the historical novels of Sir Walter Scott and fascinated by Lord Byron and his *affaires*. Her narrator is the fictitious character Lord Charles Wellesley, young brother of her Byronic hero Arthur Wellesley, Duke of Zamorna and King of Angria. Lord Charles has a habit of exposing (or, rather, re-creating) the 'truth' about his brother, partly to mystify and entertain his imaginary audience and partly to wreak revenge on Zamorna for his impatient and dismissive treatment of his younger brother. In *High Life In Verdopolis* Lord Charles focuses on Zamorna, his new queen and their entourage, treating us to a pageant of colourful characters and scenes that provide the background for a drama of deception and intrigue. In the process we, the real audience, experience the self-conscious hand of the young Charlotte Brontë as she practises the art of story-telling that will one day make her a famous novelist.

THE 'WEB' OF GLASS TOWN AND ANGRIA

The Glass Town saga is a complex creation – a web, as Charlotte herself called it, woven in childhood. *High Life In Verdopolis* is just one strand of the intricate pattern of magazines, poems, tales, fragments and even drawings constructed chiefly by Charlotte and Branwell over the years in which they matured from early adolescence to young adulthood. Charlotte was twenty-three when she wrote her last Angrian manuscript, and it can be argued that the published novels themselves owe much to her early fantasy world.

The saga began as a corporate dreamworld originally shared by the four Brontë children, Charlotte, Branwell, Emily and Anne. Like all children they acted out imaginary plays, often pretending to be famous people they had read about in local newspapers or history books. The gift of twelve toy soldiers to the nine-year-old Branwell in 1826 became the catalyst for the most famous of these games, known as the Young Men's Play. Both Charlotte and Branwell recorded the event several years later: how each of the children seized a toy soldier, named him and began weaving a fictitious world around his imaginary character. Their earliest stories document the exploits of the Twelve Adventurers, their founding of the Great Glass Town – later renamed Verdopolis – in central west Africa, and their subsequent establishment of a federation of kingdoms ruled by the four original soldiers chosen by the children.

Charlotte had named her soldier the Duke of Wellington, reflecting her father's enthusiasm for England's military hero, who was then prime minister, but it was not long before she shifted her focus from the dictatorial father figure to his more malleable sons, Arthur and Charles Wellesley. They feature as heroes in another 'play', relating the Tales of the Islanders and duplicating many of the features of the Young Men's Play. Gradually the two plays merged to form the single Glass Town saga, controlled by four guiding spirits: the Chief Genii, who were the four Brontë children themselves.

Fired by their new-found power as authors, the children became both creators of the saga and creators within the saga. Their characters took on a reality of their own, producing literature about each other, while their creators wrote more literature about the whole play. Branwell produced the first magazines and newspapers for the new society. When Charlotte took over the editorship of 'The Young Men's Magazine' her favourite characters contributed material: as the young Marquis of Douro, Arthur Wellesley submitted romantic poems, while his mischievous younger brother Lord Charles wrote satirical sketches and plays. These miniature magazines were modelled on the adult *Blackwood's Edinburgh Magazine*, whose contents were eagerly devoured by the Brontë children as each new issue arrived at the parsonage for their father.

Mr Brontë, himself the author of five volumes and a variety of newspaper contributions, treated his children as equals, allowing them unrestricted access to his library and discussing with them his literary and political interests. The result of this education can be seen in the rich allusive text of *High Life In Verdopolis*, where we find such eclectic references as the body-snatching activities of Burke and Hare, Shakespeare's *Henry IV, part 2*, and the winged horse Pegasus. Place names, titles of characters and their personalities and a myriad of other references in the saga were derived from sources as various as the Bible, the *Arabian Nights*, school geography books, classical dictionaries, histories of the Greek and Roman empires, Shakespeare, Bunyan, Milton, Wordsworth, Scott, Byron, Moore, Hogg, local newspapers and fashionable annuals. All such sources are recorded in the notes at the end of this edition.

Much of the saga was 'made out' only in talk; knowledge was

assumed between the four collaborators, who had no need to explain circumstances or background in individual stories. A self-referential world emerged, with fictitious writers and editors jockeying for authorial power over an increasingly complex and populous Glass Town society. Authors, artists, poets and critics were rapidly invented, providing each of the children with a variety of pseudonyms.

None of Emily's and Anne's early contributions to the Glass Town saga survive, and their role may have been more vocal and active than literary, though it is clear from Charlotte's early stories that their favourite characters had some influence. Gradually, however, the two younger siblings withdrew to form their own mythical world of Gondal, leaving Charlotte and Branwell in close partnership. Over the years their literary relationship fluctuated between co-operation and rivalry, eventually reaching an agreement to take the saga their own separate ways. But in the early stages, until well after *High Life In Verdopolis*, Branwell provided the lead in invention of character and plot.

Branwell was responsible for the detailed political, military and geographical features of the saga. He had a passion for documenting numbers of troops, alive or dead, as he led the Twelves and their armies in a series of wars against the native Ashantee tribes, and more than once engineered civil war in the federation. He took his cue from history lessons on the French Revolution and the recent Peninsular Wars. Inspired by the republican zeal of Napoleon, his hero Alexander Percy (alias 'Rogue') allies himself with the lower classes and leads a rebellion against the four original rulers, now the Kings of Wellington's Land, Sneakey's Land, Parry's Land and Ross's Land. Following Percy's defeat he retires to his family home in Wellington's Land and is happily married to his second wife until she dies of consumption. Disillusioned and increasingly atheistic, Percy joins the Verdopolitan army, turns traitor and is exiled for sixteen years, during which time he becomes a pirate. His stormy third marriage to Lady Zenobia Ellrington reinstates him in 'high society'. When we encounter Percy in *High Life In Verdopolis*, he is in the curious position of father-in-law to Charlotte's hero Zamorna, who has just married Mary Percy. He has recently been created Lord Northangerland and is about to be made prime minister of

Zamorna's new kingdom of Angria. Cryptic references are made in our story to Percy's former pirate life on the *Red Rover*, now an open secret in Verdopolis, and to his dark, restive personality, which becomes a pernicious influence on the younger Zamorna. Although Northangerland plays a minor role in *High Life In Verdopolis*, his love-hate relationship with Zamorna provides the central drama in the Glass Town saga. In Charlotte's early stories, Zamorna is a young Apollo – noble and talented, a poet, soldier and statesman, and fatally attractive to women. At first he is the antithesis to Northangerland, who embodies the dark side of the Byronic hero that fascinated Branwell throughout his life. As Charlotte's own reading of Byron and Shakespeare increased, her handling of her hero became more subtle. He develops a fatal flaw and an increasingly complex character: in mock desperation, Charlotte's mouthpiece – the envious Lord Charles – creates twin Zamornas in the malicious tale 'The Spell' (written in June 1834)[1] to contend with a personality and background of *affaires* and marriages spiralling out of control. Zamorna becomes power-hungry and his new acquisition of the Kingdom of Angria, won by the sword in defence of the Verdopolitan union, is his first taste of political strength against the older generation of Verdopolitan rulers, including his father. In *High Life In Verdopolis* he is a new king-in-waiting, gathering his cronies for the exodus to Angria.

HIGH LIFE IN VERDOPOLIS

The tale presented here comes midway in both the sequence of Charlotte's early manuscripts and the chronology of the Glass Town saga. It is one of the most representative of her early stories in subject, style and tone. *High Life In Verdopolis* provides an excellent introduction to Glass Town – or Verdopolitan – society and to the preoccupations of the nascent author.

The manuscript is dated 20 March 1834, almost two years after

---

[1] *An Edition of the Early Writings of Charlotte Brontë*, ed. Christine Alexander, 2 vols (Oxford: Basil Blackwell for the Shakespeare Head Press, 1987; 1991), vol. 2, part 2, p. 148.

Charlotte finished her studies at Miss Wooler's school at Roe Head, twenty miles south of Haworth, Yorkshire. Secure again in the collaborative atmosphere of Haworth Parsonage, Charlotte embarked on a period of frenetic reading, writing and drawing, indulging her thirst for knowledge and motivated by a desire for self-improvement. Her ambition at this stage was to become a professional artist, earning her living by painting miniature portraits or flowers, as her concentration on pencil and watercolour drawings suggests.[2] In 1834 she submitted two drawings of local scenes, 'Bolton Abbey' and 'Kirkstall Abbey' (both copies of engravings), for the summer exhibition of the Royal Northern Society for the Encouragement of the Fine Arts in Leeds. To see her name in *A Catalogue of The Works Of British Artists*, only eight items down from that of William Turner, whose works she had copied, must have provided tremendous encouragement. The number of detailed copies of romantic landscapes and portraits of English 'high society' that she made at this time – several of which can be seen in this volume – before returning to Roe Head as a teacher in 1835, is matched only by her prolific output of Angrian manuscripts during the same period.

It will be clear from Charlotte's illustrations included here (all except one executed within a year of *High Life In Verdopolis*), that her secret Angrian world spilled over into her more public drawing. I have recently been able to identify, for example, not only the Byronic source of one of her portraits, but also its close connection with the Glass Town poet Alexander Soult, who features in *High Life In Verdopolis* as Alphonse Soult, the Marquis of Marseilles (*see* PLATE 12). Furthermore the portrait, entitled 'Zenobia Marchioness Ellrington' (PLATE 5), Countess of Northangerland in our story, resembles the real Countess of Blessington, whose portraits frequently appeared in annuals of the period, in Heath's *Book of Beauty*, for example, and in *The Keepsake*, both of which she edited. Lady Blessington's literary career and private life accord nicely with Zenobia's role as the Glass Town blue-stocking, wife of Northangerland and platonic lover of the Duke of Zamorna. Blessington's name was constantly before the public during the

[2] *See* Christine Alexander and Jane Sellars, *The Art of the Brontës* (Cambridge: Cambridge University Press, 1995).

1830s and 1840s, and Charlotte would have been aware of her role as a London hostess, of her *ménage à trois* with her husband and the Count d'Orsay, and of her friendship with Byron in Italy. Charlotte may perhaps have read Blessington's *Journal of Conversations with Lord Byron*, which appeared in 1832 – certainly the relationship between Zenobia and Zamorna is similar to that of Blessington and Byron.

Zenobia, of course, is not simply modelled on the Countess of Blessington, but Charlotte's ready appropriation of new material from her current reading indicates the way she continually reworked her characters and their situations, constantly drawing on her latest experience, gleaned either from books or life. Zenobia was based originally on a combination of the historical Zenobia, Queen of Palmyra and the East (as recorded in Edward Gibbon's *History of the Decline and Fall of the Roman Empire*), and Madame de Staël, the noted French intellectual whom Byron referred to as the greatest mind of her times. Zenobia Ellrington is also noted for her scholarship and imposing stature; she is an accomplished author and always dresses elaborately in velvet gowns and plumed head-dresses, like those in PLATE 5.

With other characters, too, stature and dress are crucial to their definition; they reinforce Charlotte's fascination with physiognomy. It is not an accident that the young 'Fitz-Arthur' in this story so strongly resembles Zamorna, though the situation advances the plot: his features clearly reveal, to actors and audience, not only his progenitor but also the character traits he is destined to possess.

Charlotte Brontë's skill as a visual artist rests on her minute observation of detail. In her writing this facility translates into detailed vignettes of characters and vividly imagined scenes, many of which can be found in engravings of the period. When she so fondly imagines the romantic landscape of the lake district in *High Life In Verdopolis*, she has not only written of it many times before, but has also re-created it in pencil and watercolour, as in her watercolour copy of Finden's engraving of 'Bessy Bell and Mary Gray' in the *Forget Me Not* annual of 1831 (*see* PLATE 7). Both the narrator and the characters in our story view a picturesque scene or domestic interior as if they are reading a framed picture, a reflection of their young author's early training in the visual arts.

The action of the story moves from Wellesley House, home of the Duke of Wellington's family in the federal capital city of Verdopolis, to the western kingdom of Wellington's Land (later Wellingtonsland), the Glass Town equivalent of Ireland where the real Arthur Wellesley, Duke of Wellington, was born. Zamorna and his new wife make a semi-official visit to their native country before moving to Angria on the eastern borders of the federation. While Branwell was still busy finalising the details of the new kingdom – the building of the capital of Adrianopolis, planning its parliament, surveying its roads and rivers and documenting the threat of warring tribes to its borders – Charlotte preferred to linger in the past, to savour romantic love and peace while it lasted. Her characters meet to discuss plans for Angria, but their business deals are made after dinner behind closed doors, out of earshot of the reader. It is the ebb and flow of personal relations in conversation at dinner or during a ball that fascinate the gossip-mongering Lord Charles and his creator. Like Zenobia in the story, all Charlotte's characters are content to fold up their maps for another day and join the frivolities of the *haut ton*, as Charlotte refers to her select society.

The hero of this tale is Warner Howard Warner, a newcomer to the Verdopolitan scene. Born and bred in the hills of Angria, his character is more reminiscent of a straightforward Yorkshireman than of the dandified Verdopolitan nobility. Yet, as head of the oldest and most influential house in Zamorna's new kingdom, he is a necessary ally for the young monarch, and soon becomes his Home Secretary. Their relationship reflects that of the historical Duke of Wellington and Sir Robert Peel: it is founded on expediency rather than personal liking. Their characters are antipathetic, yet they respect and understand each others' strengths.

Charlotte uses this contrast in *High Life In Verdopolis* as the basis for her exploration of relations between the sexes. Warner's slight appearance (enemies term him 'hermaphrodite') and his business-like attitude to courtship are scorned by those who fawn over Zamorna's handsome person and revel in his hypocritical flirtations. The intelligent Ellen Grenville is the first of Charlotte's heroines to see past the outward man and to recognise Warner as the 'brisk gallant little cock' he is. Their repartee is reminiscent of that of Shakespeare's Beatrice and Benedick; it is the same banter that we encounter between Jane and Rochester at the end of *Jane Eyre*. But Zamorna is the unreformed, profligate, early Rochester. Charlotte is not ready to explore a more sophisticated relationship or to examine the claims of a plain heroine to passion. As we see in the opening pages of this story, she accepts (though she may not agree with) the need for beauty and a dowry if one is to experience romantic love, let alone secure a husband. Her adolescent priorities focus on those beauties who are entangled in an emotional spell 'past hope of rescue', and the unromantic courtship of Ellen and Warner is bundled into the first and last chapters.

In *High Life In Verdopolis* Charlotte systematically documents the infatuation of each of her heroines for her Byronic hero: the otherwise feminist Ellen, who feebly attempts to resist his fascination; the strong-willed Zenobia, who has long struggled against his attractions; the proud Maria Sneachie, who is subdued by the 'oriental despot'; and the faithful Mina Laury, who submits to her 'master', living in seclusion and devoting her life to the interests of her idol. Yet these episodes – significant as they are in the larger Glass Town saga – provide only a background in our story for the central relationship between Zamorna and his new bride, the brilliant Mary Percy.

This is the first appearance in Charlotte's manuscripts of the saga's central heroine. She was introduced by Branwell five months earlier in the unpublished story 'The Politics of Verdopolis' (23 October 1833), specifically referred to in *High Life In Verdopolis*. There was usually a time lag in the saga before Charlotte accepted Branwell's innovations, but Branwell recorded triumphantly at the end of his manuscript: 'NB. Highly important: Lord Charles Wellesley has condescended to say, "She is one [of] whom I can say I am pleased." ' Charlotte did not always approve of Branwell's innovations, but she seized upon Mary with delight. Zamorna had grown tired of the simple charms of his innocent wife Marion Hume, and Charlotte needed to provide him with a more challenging partnership. Yet even in this first glimpse of the newly-weds, the scene is set for Mary's constant suffering at the hands of her incurably philandering husband and his repeated absences. Unlike her predecessors, however, she is not to suffer in silence. Spirited and wilful, she is the proud daughter of Northangerland, keen to assert her rights though fearful of the wrath of her husband. In later Angrian stories she becomes the pawn in a power struggle between her father and husband, caught between the two men she loves, and although brought close to death, she survives to witness Zamorna's seduction of her young step-sister Caroline Vernon.

High Life In Verdopolis has been called 'an orgy of Byronism'.[3] The details of Byron's ancestry and even the breed of his dogs find their way into this story and are recorded in the notes at the end of this edition. Epigraphs proclaim the story's allegiance to Byron's most famous poem, *Childe Harold's Pilgrimage.* Zamorna is now an eastern potentate surrounded by his seraglio and laden with all the trappings of Byron's hero. Heroines, like Mina Laury, appropriate the actions and characters of the women Byron created and those he spurned. Engravings used to illustrate his works become visual equivalents for Charlotte's text (*see* PLATE 12). The exotic settings of his Oriental Tales and the darker side of *Manfred* or his cynical *Don Juan* are absorbed into the Angrian saga. Northangerland's past as a pirate owes much to *The Corsair*, later recalled with affection by the young Jane Eyre. Branwell – ever ready to preserve the seedy, blood-thirsty side of society – recreates his hero as demagogue, the idolized champion of the masses. In 'Real Life in Verdopolis' (May–September 1833), Percy (Northangerland) is the rampant individualist who is a law unto himself. In subsequent stories, Charlotte too provides a sordid past for Zamorna; he rivals Northangerland in ruthlessness but never develops Northangerland's disillusionment. Charlotte's increasingly critical attitude to her hero prevents the kind of introspection Branwell achieves by his close identification with Northangerland, who gradually becomes a projection of Branwell's own tormented personality.

Zamorna's appetite, it seems, is insatiable, his egotism unlimited. And although Lord Charles adopts a cynical attitude to his brother's sexual exploits, the narrative frequently lapses into an uncontrolled authorial endorsement of his behaviour. Nor can Lord Charles resist leaving us, in the final lines of his tale, with yet another titillating detail about Zamorna's past *affaires*. Charlotte herself became

[3] Fannie Ratchford in the first pioneering study of the Brontë juvenilia: *The Brontës' Web of Childhood* (New York: Columbia University Press, 1941), p. 84.

increasingly obsessed by her hero's sexual magnetism, as he replays Byron's brutality towards his wife and his ruthless manipulation of Caroline Lamb and Claire Clairmont. Not until five years after *High Life In Verdopolis* does she begin to rid herself of what had become a pathological fascination: with the creation of Elizabeth Hastings in 1839 Charlotte asserts a new morality that would eventually lead to Jane Eyre's power of conscience to resist temptation.

Yet even before she wrote *High Life In Verdopolis*, Charlotte had foreseen the conclusion of her hero's increasingly capricious and 'sphinx-like' behaviour in the political arena. In 'A Leaf from an Unopened Volume' (17 January 1834)[4] we glimpse the disastrous results of Zamorna's 'grasping and rapacious hand'. As Emperor Adrian 'the magnificent', he is to become Satan incarnate and his empire is to crumble from the corruption within: 'as if Heaven, being wrath with mankind, had sent Lucifer to reign on earth in the flesh'. Although the sequence of Charlotte's writings never reaches this predicted outcome, she and her narrator constantly warn that if the talisman of Zamorna's influence, which is seen so strongly in *High Life In Verdopolis* and which holds together so many contradictory interests, should fail, then the veil of doom will be drawn over the Glass Town saga. In *High Life In Verdopolis* we meet Zamorna at the beginning of the end, and we observe his increasingly voluptuous and despotic nature.

THE MANUSCRIPT

The manuscript consists of 23 pages (18.5 × 11 cm) of a hand-sewn booklet, written in the close minuscule script that is typical of all the Brontës' early writings. It has been bound in a handsome black morocco binding (*see* p. ix), together with 'The Spell, An Extravaganza' and 'The Scrap Book. A Mingling of Many Things', both written by Lord Charles Wellesley three months after *High Life In Verdopolis*. The bound manuscript volume, enclosed in a slip case, is now in the British Library (Add. MS. 34255).

Facsimiles of four manuscript pages are included in this volume.

---

[4] *An Edition of the Early Writings of Charlotte Brontë*, vol. 2, part 1, p. 321.

It will be evident to the reader that the dashes which are often said to be a significant feature of Charlotte Brontë's early, so-called 'headlong' style, are seldom found in this novelette. The impression conveyed by the type of deletions and corrections made in *High Life In Verdopolis* is one of hesitation and, at times, even lack of concentration. The mistakes are frequently those made when copying an earlier draft; for example, there is a high percentage of words or phrases that are repeated and then crossed through (*see* 'rich & luxurious ~~luxurious~~ furniture' near the foot of MS. page 1 in PLATE 1).

The manuscript is neatly written; it was intended to be a fair copy, although Charlotte constantly improved her text almost as soon as she had written it. Many corrections are written immediately after a deletion on the same line, others are written above the deletion to improve a phrase or add a more appropriate word, such as the corrections at the beginning of Chapter I where 'Africa's' is substituted for 'Belgium's' (the country in the original Byronic quotation: *see* note 3, page 87), 'excites' replaces 'accelerates', and the less pretentious 'met with' and 'high' are substituted for 'fixed upon' and 'lofty' respectively (*see* PLATE 1).

High Life In Verdopolis was never intended to be published, but it was preserved by Charlotte, together with other early manuscripts that document her fantasy world. It is clear that she considered this particular novelette as one of her more successful productions, since it was among those she selected to take to Brussels to show her French teacher, Constantin Heger, George MacLean, who first records the history of the manuscript in his edition of *The Spell: An Extravaganza* (London: Oxford University Press, 1931), suggests that the manuscripts may either have been left at the Pensionnat Heger when Charlotte and Emily hastily returned to England in November 1842, after hearing news of the death of their Aunt, or may have been brought back to Brussels with Charlotte when she returned for a second year. They were then left in the keeping of Heger, who probably bound them after the success of *Jane Eyre*, as evidence of the work of his most distinguished pupil.

The appearance of the little leather volume on a second hand bookstall in Brussels in the early 1890s is curious, since Heger did not die until 1896. However there were changes at the Pensionnat after the death of his wife in 1890, which may account for its sale. We owe the discovery of the manuscript to Professor Ernest Nys of the University of Brussels, who wrote to the British Museum for a valuation in 1892, and subsequently sold the volume to the Museum on 10 October.

Thus *High Life In Verdopolis* was one of the few early Brontë manuscripts that were not taken to Ireland by Charlotte Brontë's husband, the Reverend Arthur Bell Nicholls, when he returned to his family home in Banagher, in 1861. It was safely in the British Museum when Clement Shorter, acting as an agent for Thomas James Wise, made his famous purchase of Brontë manuscripts from Nicholls in 1895. Consequently it escaped the notorious machinations of Wise, who was not only responsible for many early unreliable transcriptions, but also caused the deliberate fragmentation of a number of unpublished Brontë manuscripts.[5] *High Life In Verdopolis* remained intact and unedited until four years ago when it was published for the first time in the present editor's multi-volume *Edition of the Early Writings of Charlotte Brontë*, vol. 2, part 2 (Oxford: Basil Blackwell, 1991).

THE TEXT OF THE PRESENT EDITION

The text of the present edition is based on a new transcription of the manuscript and is a compromise between readability and the desire to preserve as much as possible of the original manuscript.

The central challenge for an editor of Brontë juvenilia is how best to translate the informal and idiosyncratic nature of the manuscripts into print. It is impossible to represent in type an original handwritten manuscript, yet the layout of the Brontë manuscripts with their detailed title pages, prefaces, interpolations and postscripts, is crucial to their interpretation. Charlotte Brontë was especially

---

[5] For an account of Wise's handling of Brontë's manuscripts, see Christine Alexander, *A Bibliography of the Manuscripts of Charlotte Brontë* (Haworth and New York: The Brontë Society in association with Meckler Publishing, 1982), pp. xvi-xvii; and Victor A. Neufeldt (ed.), *The Poems of Charlotte Brontë: A New Text and Commentary* (New York and London: Garland Publishing, Inc., 1985), pp. xxii-xxxiii.

concerned with the visual aspect of the preliminary pages of her manuscripts, as illustrated on page i which simulates the original title page of *High Life In Verdopolis*. She was less concerned, however, with the mechanics of punctuation, which is haphazard throughout the manuscript. Nor did she separate the story into paragraphs: she wrote this tale as she did many of her novelettes, as a continuous text broken only by chapter headings and occasional verses.

The problem of authentic presentation of the text is compounded when the aim of the edition, as in the present case, is to reach a wide audience keen to read Charlotte Brontë's early stories, but reluctant to wade through intrusive editorial symbols that describe within the text the various additions and emendations she made. Often such complicated scholarly apparatus simply confuses the reader. Nor does the preservation of Charlotte's often meaningless punctuation assist in the accessibility of the text or facilitate the enjoyment of the reader. On the other hand, the publication of a single Brontë manuscript presents a special opportunity to preserve the original text in ways that would not be possible in a multi-volume edition of all her early writings.

With these issues in mind, editorial intervention has been kept to a minimum. The aim is to present the reader with a clear text that still conveys the flavour of this early personal writing. The layout of the original manuscript with its title page, chapter headings, epigraphs and dates has been preserved, but paragraphs have been introduced into what would otherwise be unbroken text within each chapter. Charlotte Brontë's grammatical irregularities and original spelling (including both archaisms and errors) and her inconsistent word division (for example, the use of both 'bluebell' and 'bluebell', 'forever' and 'for ever') and use of ampersand ('&') have been preserved. Even the erratic capitalisation has been retained, except at the beginning of sentences where Charlotte Brontë's lower case letters have been made upper case.

Complete retention of the manuscript punctuation, however, would undoubtedly obscure the content of the text and bewilder the reader. Approximately a third of the sentences in the manuscript end without punctuation, or they are strung together by a series of commas. Inverted commas often open but fail to close a sentence, or one set of inverted commas both closes one sentence and opens the next. Thus, the manuscript punctuation has been retained where possible but otherwise normalized. Occasional editorial comments are made in square brackets and uncertain readings are placed in square brackets with a question mark.

The selected facsimile pages of the manuscript have been placed as near to the relevant text as possible so that the reader can see the few differences between this text and the original. A short list of deletions, corrections and additions found in these manuscript pages is included at the back of this edition; those who wish to reconstruct further Charlotte Brontë's changes of mind in the process of composition are advised to consult the textual notes of the present editor's *Edition of the Early Writings of Charlotte Brontë*, vol. 2, part 2.

An important aspect of the present edition is the annotation, which provides a context for *High Life In Verdopolis*. The introduction is designed to relate the story both to the Brontës' own imaginary world and to the cultural and literary milieu of the period, but the Notes to the Text, at the end of this edition, illustrate in detail Charlotte Brontë's familiarity with other literary texts and the self-reflexive nature of her own writings. The same characters reappear throughout her early manuscripts, sometimes under a new name or in a different guise; references are often made to previous stories or poems, political or sexual scandals, battles or business deals, and the young author often experiments with different literary genres or personae. All these features must be recorded if the reader is to appreciate the rich intertextuality and the vivid realisation of the enclosed world of Glass Town and Angria. Read in combination, the text and annotation of *High Life In Verdopolis* provide a glimpse into the multifarious world of Charlotte Brontë's 'web of childhood'.

High Life
in
Verdopolis, or

The difficulties of annexing
a suitable title to a work
practically illustrated in
Six
Chapters. ~
By Lord C A F
Wellesley[1]

Much cry and little wool, as St
Nicholas said when he was
shearing the Hog.[2]

motto ~

March 20th 1834 ~

CHAPTER THE Ist

A Gladder day usurped the place of night
For Africa's Capital had gathered then
Her beauty & her chivalry & bright
The lamps shone o'er fair women & brave men.[3]

I like high life. I like its manners, its splendors, its luxuries, the beings which move in its enchanted sphere. I like to consider the habits of those beings, their way of thinking, speaking, acting. Let fools talk about the artificial, voluptuous, idle existences spun out by Dukes, Lords, Ladies, Knights & Squires of high degree. Such cant is not for me; I despise it. What is there of artificial in the lives of our Verdopolitan Aristocracy? What is there of idle? Voluptuous they are to a proverb: splendidly, magnificently voluptuous, but not inactive, not unnatural. Look at Northangerland[4] — who among the race of plodding plebeians equals him in laborious & ceaseless energy? I say not whether his toils have been in the broad & downward, or the narrow & ascending path;[5] but I point merely to the Fact of the unlimited labour, the wild & weighty work he has performed since manhood's down first began to roughen his chin. Look at Fidena,[6] at Thornton,[7] at Warner,[8] at Castlereagh,[9] at Lofty (the dead, I mean, not the living viscount)[10] & tell me a vulgar name which distinguished itself more than those illustrious appellations during the late hard-fought war. They lie still till Glory calls, but then they awake; & in the struggle for fame it is seen whether lordly or low-born blood excites to greater exertions the heart & limbs, which are animated by the crimson current, be it clear or muddy.

The above passage is extracted from an article in a later number of Tree's *Verdopolitan magazine*,[11] which from internal evidence is known to be the production of Zamorna's impetuous pen.[12] I adopt it for the commencement of my present work, not because the tone of feeling which dictated it meets my approval, but because it serves well as an introduction to a book which treats principally of lords, ladies, Knights and Squires of high degree, &

whose first scene is placed in the breakfast-room of Warner Hotel, situated in the highly aristocratic region of Ebor Terrace.[13] Here, on a drizzly morning about the middle of February 1834,[14] sat Warner Howard Warner Esq[r], engaged in reading the batch of post-meridian papers which usually forms one of the component parts of a gentleman's morning meal. The delicate vessel of porcelain stood beside him, half-filled with chocolate; a dozen Golden plover's eggs rested on a fine damask napkin; the silver coffee urn steamed above a mat of embroidered velvet; & these elegant breakfast appointments, arranged on [a] round rose-wood table, formed the central ornaments of a room whose mingled magnificence & comfort might have satisfied even the critical fastidiousness of my friend General Thornton.[15]

But Warner's meal was not solitary. Two other persons partook it with him. One of these — a lady somewhat advanced in years, of slight & low form, but refined & high-bred demeanour — was his mother. The other, before whom the coffe & chocolate equipage was placed, & who with much grace discharged the duty of distributing the good things at her command, was likewise a female, apparently not more than eighteen years old. The striking likeness visible in her youthful features to Warner, indicated her to be what she was, his sister, & I believe the youngest of the Family. An almost unbroken silence was maintained while he continued engaged in the perusal of the newspapers, but as he laid the last down his mother addressed him thus:

"Warner," said she, "when do you intend to leave Verdopolis? I am tired of its noise & bustle & long to be back at the old Hall."

"Leave Verdopolis!" exclaimed the young lady before her brother had time to reply. "Leave Verdopolis Mother! Why, we have scarcely been here more than two months & I have not yet had time to wear off my astonishment & begin to feel unmixed delight. Besides, you wished Warner to be married before he returned to the Hall, & I don't think he has met with any-one yet whom he thinks worthy to receive the honour of his name."

This was said in a lower tone & with a sly glance towards her brother.

"Well," said M[rs] Warner, "I must say I wished my son to carry back to the Estate a lady for his tenants & retainers, but as you say,

Theresa, I don't perceive that he has yet thought seriously of the circumstance. Are we right Warner?"

"Perfectly so, madam. I have been too much engaged since my arrival in this city to think of marriage, but as I consider such an event warranted by prudence & urged by necessity, I shall begin to consider it more deeply than I have done."

"That's right, brother," said Theresa, rising from her chair & going towards him. "Now tell me what kind of wife you would like to have. Should she be very handsome?"

"Why, yes. Sufficiently so to please myself."

"Very accomplished?"

"The same answer will do as that I gave your former question."

"Very rich?"

Warner nodded.

"Of Good family?"

"Unquestionably."

"Of Graceful manners?"

"Most asuredly."

"Young?"

"Yes."

"Of Good temper?"

"Aye," he replied quickly, "that is absolutely necessary, for she must bear with me."

"Well," said Theresa, "I think I have exhausted my catalogue of qualities. Now let me see: Young, rich, handsome, graceful, accomplished & good tempered. Brother, you require too much! I do not know where you will find a wife gifted with all these requisites."

"Oh never trouble *your* head about the matter, my sage sister. I can manage for myself."

"I don't doubt it, Warner. But still, just listen to my advice, it can do you no harm. Tomorrow is Wednesday & in the evening we go to the Grand Party at Wellesley House. There will be assembled all the principal ladies in Verdopolis. Make your choice then. It will be a fair opportunity of seeing & comparing."

Warner made no answer but by again desiring Theresa to mind her own affairs. But in his heart he thought her counsel apropos enough & determined to follow it.

There is something highly impressive to me in the appearance which a suite of noble appartments presents when all lighted & arranged for the reception of company, before the bustle of annunciations and arrivals has yet commenced. I enjoyed the spectacle in perfection on the Wednesday evening above alluded to, for, happening to be at Wellesley House, I came down from my chamber as soon as I was dressed & accompanied Mrs Temple in her survey of the rooms after the house-maids had completed their labours. With a slow tread & a critical eye the stately Dame moved on, through all the vista of proud saloons, glowing with brilliant fires & dazzling chandeliers, whose warm ruddy beams slept on rich carpets, silken sofas, cushions, ottomans, Gleaming groups of statuary, sideboards where the flash of plate & glass almost blinded the eye that gazed on them, ample tables covered with splendid engravings, portfolios, magnificently bound volumes, Gold musical boxes, enamelled miniature vases, Guitars of elaborate & beautiful workmanship, clocks & lamps of alabaster & ormolu, &c., &c., &c. Yet notwithstanding the immense quantity of rich & luxurious furniture, disposed with such exquisite taste in those lordly halls, yet so vast was their size & so high their gilded ceilings, that in their present state of solitude the steps & voices of myself & Mrs Temple awoke a very audible echo whenever we spoke or moved.

Whilst I ran about shouting to rouse the Daughter of the Arch[16] & listening to her faint voice as it died away along cornice & surfase, the lady-house-keeper walked more sedately on. At each table, sideboard, mirror, & pedestal, she paused, passed her finger over the polished surface &, if the slightest soil proclaimed the presence of dust, however light & recent, wiped it carefully with a delicate white cambrick handkerchief which she carried in one hand, at the same time not forgetting to comment pretty sharply on the slovenliness of the house-maids. Having at length finished her scrupulous survey, she informed me that she was about to quit the appartments.

"And lord Charles," said she, "I insist upon your following me, for I dare not leave you here alone. It makes me shudder to see you approach those mirrors in such a headless[17] manner, when you must be aware of their great value & brittle materials."

Not being inclined to obey her commands, I set off at a run, knowing that she was far too grave & staid to think of pursuing me. She, however, summoned one of the footmen who had already taken their stations on the grand staircase and at the Entrances, and by his assistance I was speedily caught. Seeing that just indignation at such grossly insulting treatment was exciting me both to tears & exclamations, Mrs Temple now endeavoured to soothe the fiery temper which she had aroused.

"Hush my lord," said she in a low & anxious tone, "for heaven's sake be silent or his Grace will hear you & then — "[18]

"Hang his Grace!" was my unhesitating reply. "What do I care for either him or you? Let me go, woman, this instant, or I'll give you that you'll not soon be the better of!"

"Come darling," she continued, still endeavouring to appease the irritated Lion, "don't be so angry with me or I shall begin to cry also. There, that's right, wipe your eyes & go to the Duchess;[19] she's in her dressing-room & will be glad of your company till the carriages begin to arrive, I dare say."

No one has a more placable & amiable disposition than myself. Therefore, seeing that Mrs Temple was now sorry for the disrespect she had been guilty of towards my person, I consented to forgive her, as she is a Good Lady in the main, though at times given to forget the homage due to my rank and merits. Accompanying her then in her departure from the saloons, I hastened to my sister-in law's dressing-room. Gently, & at the same time, with something of a flourish, I delivered three raps on the door.

"Who is there?" asked the sweet & cheerful tones of her Grace, the Duchess.

"Your Servant, madam. Lord Charles Wellesley."

"Come in, my little sweetheart," was the reply.

Thus invited, I opened the door & entered Mary Henrietta's Sanctum Sanctorum,[20] to which I don't think even Zamorna himself would have been admitted at that hour. She was sitting at her Glass attired in a loose & graceful undress, half-reclined on a sort of settee. An open book lay on the toilette table before her amidst a dazzling profusion of rings, jewels & ornaments of various kinds, & her beautiful slender white hand was placed on the leaves to keep them in their expanded position. Her two favourite waiting maids, Mrs Frances Ellis & Mrs Jane Graham, were likewise in the room, the former engaged in arranging the bright profusion of her lady's auburn curls & the latter in completing some article of dress.

"Well Charles," said the divine Duchess, kissing me as I approached her, "you are come to keep me company whilst I dress I suppose. You are welcome, love, but remember, few besides yourself possess the privelige of entering my dressing room. Fanny! hand lord Wellesley a chair."

Miss Ellis immediately brought forward a comfortable cushioned fauteuil,[21] into which she assisted me to mount, & when I was settled I proceeded to answer Mary thus: "I am, my dear, fully sensible of the distinction with which you constantly treat me, & it gives me real & heartfelt pleasure to find that in the present age of almost universal frivolity there is still one remaining so young, admired & gifted as yourself who knows the deference due to genuine worth. All pleasures are, however, mingled with some alloy of pain, & in proportion to my estimate of your value is my regret at the circumstance of such a treasure being in the possession of the reprobate ne'er-do weel,[22] my brother. I hope, my dear, he behaves to you with kindness & constancy. If not, pray inform me & I shall know how to punish him!"

With these words I turned to Mary. I am sorry to say that there was an expression about her beautiful mouth as if she were trying to suppress a laugh. She did, however, restrain it & answered with tolerable gravity, "Thank you, lord Charles, for your knightly offer, which, however, I do not at present mean to accept. But if ever I have any grievances to redress you shall be my champion."

"Hark!" she continued, "I hear a carriage. Jane, is my dress ready? The bells are tolling half past nine."

At that instant the silver chime of St Augustin's Cathedral & the gong-like & more distant bell of St Michael's[23] rung out in unison with the rattle of approaching wheels.

"My lady," replied Miss Graham, "I have scarcely twelve stitches to put in. It will be done directly."

"Never mind Girl," said her indulgent young mistress, "don't hurry yourself so. I can wear some other gown. Fetch me the dark maroon satin one, Fanny."

PLATE I: First page of Chapter I of the manuscript
'High Life In Verdopolis'.

PLATE 2: 'Portrait of a young woman', c.1833-1834; pencil and crayon drawing by Charlotte Brontë, suggestive of Mary Henrietta Percy, wife of Zamorna and Queen of Angria. By courtesy of the Brontë Society.

"O, no my lady, I have finished now," said Jane as she fastened the silk & broke it off. "And this deep shaded green & violet is just the colour his Grace likes; it becomes you exquisitely," she continued as she & her fellow maiden arrayed Mary in the rich & splendid garment. In ten minutes she was dressed, & most lovely did she look, with the dark changing folds of the silk falling round her slender form, no necklace or other ornaments encircling her snowy and swanlike neck, but a priceless gem in her bosom & in her ears two diamond rings, long, trembling, clear & pendant as drops of crystalline summer dew.

She now left her dressing-room &, accompanied by myself, proceeded to the saloons. Several carriages had arrived during this interim, & on entering the first saloon we found near twenty persons assembled. Mary Henrietta bowed to her guests with the noble Grace proper to Zamorna's Wife & Northangerland's daughter. She conversed with them a few moments & then passed on to the next apartment; here we found only General Thornton.

"Ha, my lady," said he, advancing to shake hands according to his custom, "I have to accuse you of being deficient in punctuality. Nine o'clock precisely was the time mentioned on the invitation cards: it's now near ten, & you've only just entered the rooms. What have you to say for such remissness?"

"I must plead guilty," replied the Duchess with a smile, "but my little champion lord Wellesley can tell you the delay was owing to no fault of mine."

I of course substantiated her appeal, & Thornton went on talking for sometime of the advantages of punctuality & the misfortunes incident to delay. At length the Duchess, who is not accustomed to put much guard over her feelings, because from her childhood her slightest expressed wish was sufficient to sanction the removal of whatever might be annoying or unpleasant to her, began to exhibit symptoms of impatience at the worthy General's prolixity. He perceived it &, with much politeness, brought his exhortation to a brief conclusion &, as the Duchess rose to go away, offered her his arm as a support. She was just about to accept it when the loud annunciation from the other appartment of the Duke & Duchess of Fidena stopped her. Thornton looked offended & muttered something about other Folks being no better worth pleasing than himself.[24]

"My dear General," said Mary Henrietta with the sweetest deprecating look in the world, "now don't be angry. You know Prince John is my lord's friend & I dare not offend him."

"Very well my lady," replied Thornton, who was instantly pacified by her sweet smile & by the cordiality with which she put her white hand into his. "Its all right I dare say & I was a fool to grumble about the matter."

At this instant the Royal pair entered from the first saloon, followed by the little marquis of Rosendale.[25] A stately yet friendly greeting passed between them & the duchess, & Fidena then apologized slightly for bringing his son, saying that he was so anxious to come that his mother had found it impossible to deny him.

"Kiss me," said Augustus, coming up to Mary. "I met Zamorna in the hall & he said I was to ask you for two kisses: one for me & one for himself."

Mary Henrietta threw herself on to an ottoman, snatched up the beautiful & noble child in her arms, & regardless of her rich dress & elaborate tresses, kissed & fondled him with enthusiastic tenderness. At length, as if suddenly recollecting herself, she started up.

"What have I done?" said she, turning to a large mirror. "Rumpled my dress & disordered my hair! O Fanny Ellis would break her heart if she were to see her handiwork so destroyed by a moment's imprudence!"

"Let the curls alone," said her Grace of Fidena. "They look better than ever. Yet you should remember not to play with my boy in full dress." Mary did at this moment look most enchanting; the glow on her countenance, the beautiful disarrangement of her hair & the glance of something like upbraiding with which she regarded the laughing Augustus as he said shrewdly enough for one of his age of five years, "How many of those kisses were for my god-father?" invested her with irresistible fascination.

At this moment the Duke entered, accompanied by the earl & countess Northangerland,[26] Lord & lady Castlereagh, Mr & Miss Montmorency,[27] my aunt lady Somers,[28] my cousin Julia,[29] the Earl & Countess of St Clair,[30] & a host of equally noble & distinguished personages.

"Zamorna! Zamorna!" exclaimed lord Rosendale, running towards him as he stood in the midst of the briliant train. "The Duchess has sent you twenty kisses instead of one. Bend down that I may give them to you."

"Nay," said Arthur, patting the little thing's curly head, "I won't be kissed by proxy, Augustus. Tell my lady she must perform that ceremony in person, a substitute will scarcely do." Augustus ran to do his errand & the Duke & his party passed on, laughing at the child's naïvetè.

And now the tide of arrivals reached its flood; carriage after carriage dashed & drew up at the grand entrance & their contents, consisting of all the grace, elegance, fashion & haut-ton[31] of Verdopolis, soon overflowed the floors of the sumptuous saloons with a dazzling & bewildering throng of African aristocrats. Amongst these was Mr Warner, to whom I must now recur as the hero of my tale.

After having received & returned the greeting of his fair & noble hostess, he zealously set about the business for which he was come: namely, that of exam[in]ing the female portion of the company, with a view of discovering which of them was best fitted to form a partner & associate for himself. In so doing, he was actuated by the plainest & most common-life motives imaginable. Not a particle of romance, not a spark of enthusiasm, influenced his thoughts on the subject or exagerated his conceptions regarding the sort of person whose hand, heart & fortune he would condescend to unite with his own. Slowly & deliberately he walked up the appartment towards the fireplace, near which an attractive group of sweet young ladies were amusing themselves by turning over a portfolio of drawings.

Warner sat down a short distance from them; his restless, bright & penetrating eye wandered with searching rapidity over the laughing cluster of fair ones. On six of the party it dwelt only for an instant, but on the seventh it made a longer stay. This was a smiling, rosy girl with brown hair & dark eyes. She knelt before the sofa on which the rest were seated & distributed to them the pictures from the portfolio. This she did with an air not so remarkable for swiming grace as for nature & sprightliness, talking all the while rather rapidly & with an accent not perfectly English, but with a tone of voice so sweet, clear & animating that it quite took captive Mr Warner's ear & through that almost stole to his heart.

"Blanche, be quick!" said she, addressing one of her companions. "I'm tired of waiting for you; that picture has grown quite stale & here is another far better. But listen! I hear the music; so no more poring over drawings." So saying, she threw down the portfolio, scattered its contents about, & bounded away with the light step of a roe.

"Who is that interesting Girl?" inquired Warner of his Sister Theresa, who happened at that instant to be standing near him.

"Lady Flora Roslyn," was her reply.

"What's in a name?"[32] asks some one. It should seem a great deal, for no sooner had these three simple words been uttered, than the expression of incipient admiration which had begun to dawn on our Hero's tranquil features dyed entirely away, the sparkle of his eye disappeared, a faint "Pshaw" escaped his lips & with a cold look of the most perfect indifference he folded his arms & sank back in his chair.

Reader, as a reason for this transformation, be pleased to remember that lady Flora Roslyn is the daughter of lord St Clair. That nobleman's estates are entailed & consequently the Ladies of his family will have to seek their fortunes by marriage and not bring a dowry to him with whom they may be united. After Warner had spent about ten minutes in gulping down this disappointment, he rose & proceeded to the dancing-room. Here he found about fifty couples engaged in threading the mazes of the rapid & graceful waltz. Silently stationing himself among the number of the by-standers, he listened for some time to the soft inspiring strains of the orchestra & the cheerful hum of voices round him rapt in a kind of pleasing reverie. From this a gentle tap on the shoulder shortly waked him.

He turned round. Two ladies stood at his elbow, whose tall & noble forms, jetty tresses, & ample brows announced the princesses Edith & Maria Sneachi.[33] To his low & respectful obeisance the former only replied by a stately bow & a single glance of her bright but solemn eyes. Something like a smile dawned, too, on the rich lip, but it faded instantly & gave place to the usual cold, sad & almost severe expression, with which hopes blighted in the bud & deep heart corroding sorrow, acting on a mind whose hereditary pride & natural susceptibility made it but too well calculated to receive & retain strong impressions, have invested her youthful & handsome features.

Far different was the bearing of Maria. "Ah, Mr Warner," said she, lifting her finger with an air of arch raillery, "absent I perceive. What now might have been the subject of your thoughts: love, war or politics? In the two latter sciences I know you are an adept, but in the former by all accounts as yet only a neophyte — nay, scarcely that, I am told. However, you are now in a fair school of instruction provided you only possess the disposition to profit by what you learn. What of your abilities, Sir, are they apt or dull?"

"My lady," replied Warner, "I can hardly answer your question with correctness, the trial to which I am now put is not fair. With such a teacher as the Princess Maria, an idiot might soon become a master in the Art of love."

"Come," said she, "you have already advanced a step. I never heard you compliment before, Sir, but we will not overburden our disciple with too many lessons at once, so for the present, farewell."

So saying, she took her sister's arm & both turned to depart. Warner gazed after them with a glance so sharp & keen that it seemed as if his rapt soul were sitting in his eyes. He followed them a few steps with an almost involuntary movement, but suddenly paused as the following words struck his ear: "Edith, I could soon fool that semi-hermaphrodite to the top of his bent, & I would do it, only I am afraid of John's anger."

"By heaven, but she shall not!" exclaimed Warner half-aloud, while his fair & smooth forehead was contracted with the frown of an incensed Giant.

"Were you addressing me, Sir?" asked the calm & deliberate voice of Sir Robert Pelham.[34]

Our hero looked up. His eyes met the politician's placid & unmoved countenance, whose expression was so at variance with the roused & stinging irritation which now agitated his own mind.

[*13*]

Giving way to the impulse of the moment, he delivered a stunning blow on the baronet's smiling mouth.

"My God!" he exclaimed, reeling back while the blood gushed from his wounded gums. "What is that for?"

"To teach you the doctrine of non-interference," replied Warner.

"Of course, sir, you will see the necessity of making an apology to my friend," said Sir John Flower,[35] who at that moment stept up.

"Does he require it?" asked Warner.

"Most assuredly, Sir," replied Pelham, again advancing. "And I trust you will not be imprudent enough to refuse it, otherwise I shall feel it incumbent on me to demand satisfaction of another kind."

"Sir Robert, Sir Robert," said a soft voice close at hand. "You will not persist in what you have just said. Retract it I beg, nay I command, for in my own house I have a right to do so."

"My lady," replied Sir Robert turning to the Duchess of Zamorna, for it was she who spoke, "at your request I would do much, but in this affair —"

"Nay, no exceptions. Will you not yield when I implore you?"

"I will," said Pelham, in a tone of more emotion than I ever heard him use before, "I will — be the consequences what they may," & with these words he strode off.

"The English Coward," muttered lord William Lennox,[36] who with a host of puppies similar to himself had gathered round to witness the dispute.

Mary Henrietta turned to him; the ample Percy Forehead grew dark & the fully bright hazel eye lightened with anger as she said, "That sentence does no honour either to your head or heart, Sir."

"Hey," growled the rebuked nobleman, "I wish Zamorna were here to see all this interest in the discarded lover."

"I am here," said the Duke, stepping forward like a raised apparition into the circle where his wife stood.

Lennox was frightened at the spirit which he had conjured & wished to retire, but Zamorna's eye was on him.

"Leave the house, sir," he said in a firm but quick tone.

Lord William hesitated, buttoned & unbottoned his coat, blustered a little, but finally seemed to consider obedience as the most prudent course, for turning on his heel he made a reluctant & brusque retreat amidst the jeers & laughter of his companions.

"Now madam," continued my brother, "what has occasioned all this unpleasant confusion?"

Warner here advanced & briefly related the circumstances of the case.

"Very well," he said, "I am satisfied." But the cold & haughty smile with which he regarded his lady & the gloom which came across his forehead spoke otherwise. Mary observed this appearance of deep displeasure; her face grew as white as death & sick with agitation. She dropped into a chair which stood near. The ladies now gathered round for the purpose of assisting her, for her languid eye & colourless cheek seemed to presage a swoon. Zamorna did not stir. He continued quietly gazing at her with folded arms & a most strange & chilling expression of countenance. Erelong, by the application of vinaigrettes, fans, &c., &c., she revived. Rising slowly & with her hand motioning away the throng which had assembled on all sides, she moved forward a step or two towards her husband, but stopped irresolutely when she had come within a yard of him.

"Are you better?" he asked drily & coldly.

The tears started into her eyes & she looked reproachfully at the disdainful & jealous Despot. Restraining her emotion, however, & speaking in a low tone with as much indifference as she could, she answered, "A little, my lord, but the heat of the room still oppresses me."

"Does it?" he said. "Come this way then," & striding to a window he drew aside the silken curtain which hung before it, flung up the sash & beckoned [her] to sit down on a chair which one of the gentlemen hastened to hand her. "Now," he continued, turning to the company, "what is the reason of this silence & gloom? Let the orchestra strike up & the dancers return to their places. Is the mirth to be displaced & the good meeting broken with most detested disorder, by the mere rumour & first breath of a brawl? I hope not. Come, lady Maria. You & I will show a better example. Musicians play your merriest measure!"

With these words he led forth the handsome & brillant daughter of Alexander,[37] whose cheek glowed with the brightest blush of pleasure as the irresistible Zamorna whirled her away to the giddy & wheeling waltz with a cavalier-like unceremoniousness that none but his omnipotent & audacious self dared have used towards a princess of the blood.

All, now inspired by the joyous music & the example of their entertainer, threw off the spell which had begun to steal over them & mingled cheerfully in the genial pleasure of the dance or the more placid enjoyment of conversation. But amidst the hum of happy voices, the strains of animating melody, the glow of lights, the glitter of gems & the waving of plumes, I looked to Mary as she sat alone by the still open lattice, her clustered curls stirred at intervals by the balmy African night-wind, her beautiful & spotless forehead resting on her delicate hands & her eyelids closed seemingly by the heaviness of a sorrowful heart. The sight reminded me of "the vision for ever, ever vanished"[38] & I could scarcely restrain my tears.

"Lovely Creature," thought I, "is your doom to be as dark as that of her who went before you?[39] Must that haughty Serpent, concealing under his glittering & crested pride a sting of such deadly venom, number you also among his victims? Look! There is another bright bird caught in the basilisk's fascination.[40] Ah! Lady Maria, lady Maria, beware! Don't listen to his voice: when the tones are sweetest, the danger is darkest. Don't gaze on his smiles: when they are most winning your Good Genius would most earnestly summon you to take heed before it is too late. Your coquetry & disdain have brought many to despair; what if yourself should at length suffer the torments which you have often inflicted?"

Whilst I moralized thus, Arthur & his royal partner left the dance & retired to a sofa. They sat for sometime in conversation, but erelong I saw the Duke's dark eye steal towards the window where his wife yet remained. Probably he was struck by the awful resemblance above alluded to, for suddenly he rose & advanced towards her. The deep embayment of the window & the rich fall of crimson drapery on each side screened him & her from the observation of the rest of the party, but I who was stationed nearer than they thought could see & hear all that past between them. Zamorna came on with his lightest tread; he folded his arms & rested them around the back of her chair, then bending down till his lips almost touched her said in that beguiling undertone of his which was given him to entice —

> My lady turned her from the light
> Which filled her radiant halls
> To where through veil and shade of night
> The dying moon-beam falls.
> Why does she leave the dance & song,
> The sweet harp's stirring tone?
> Why turns she from the glittering throng
> To sigh & mourn alone?

Mary turned round, took the hand which was now laid on her shoulder, kissed it fondly & replied with admirable tact —

> She dreamt she saw a glance of fire
> Shot forth from princely eyes,
> And viewed the scarlet flush of ire
> To brow of marble rise.
> The troubling dream is past & over:
> Beloved, *thy* love will sigh no more.

"Bless thee," said the Duke laughing. "Why, Mary, thou art a poetess. But come, *my* love, will you leave the window or is the heat still too oppressive?"

"Nay, lordly minstrel, noble poet, my own Zamorna, I will follow you, & you must not smile at me again so scornfully as you did just now, or I shall burst out as the Italians say 'a dirotto pianto'[41] in spite of myself."

"Yes, if you give me cause," said the Duke suddenly grasping her arm with vehemence, "I will smile at you ten times more scornfully [?as] I will upbraid you with such bitterness that your heart shall break while listening to me. Henrietta, I am infernally jealous. Did you know that part of my character before we were married?"

[*17*]

"I guessed it, my lord."

"Then you were not taken by surprise to-night."

"No, yet I was unconscious that what I did could in any way incur your displeasure."

"Hush, love, don't attempt to extenuate. Leave your husband, Mary, to find out his own faults if he has done wrong, & never either by inference or direct assertion show him w[h]ere they lie." He then drew her arm through his & led her away to join the rest of the party.

But it is now time to return to Mr Warner. After the fracas with Sir Robert Pelham, he left the dancing room as its cheerful gaitey no way assorted with the angry nature of his present mood. Wandering thoughtfully along he found himself, almost before he was aware, at the entrance of a kind of inner drawing-room, where the exclusive and personal friends of Zamorna & his lady were gathered in a small but select knot.

"I shall have quiet here at least," said Warner as he removed the screen which veiled the door-way & introduced himself into the choice cluster of aristocrats. He had no sooner taken his seat than his eye was attracted by a lady of remarkably fascinating appearance. She was both young & handsome, but her chief charm was derived from the air of une femme comme il faut[42] which was diffused over her whole person. There was all the elegance, the inimitable ease, the aspect of acknowledged superiority which distinguishes a leader of the beau monde. Her features, it is true, wore the paleness of dissipation & her manner was altogether something languid & ennuyè,[43] but still she looked unspeakably lovely. She was seated on a sofa beside the Earl of Northangerland, with whom she conversed at intervals in a low & peculiarly soft tone. When Warner entered, he had apparently been asking her to dance, for she was just replying, "No, my lord, I can't. It is such a fatiguing exercise & that wild Zamorna, if he sees me stand up for a minuet or quadrille, is sure to call for the very quickest & liveliest air he can think of."[44]

"Will you have a game of chess then, my lady?" said the earl.

"Ah, that is the best plan you have thought of yet. I think I will. General Thornton, may I trouble you to bring the chess-board?"

The General instantly handed it forward & with great good nature arranged the chess-men on their respective chequers, assigning the white ones to the lady & the red ones to Northangerland. The former now seemed to kindle into something like interest. She raised herself from her half-recumbent position on the sofa, opened her languid blue eyes & bent her fair brow with an expression of thought. The Earl, on the contrary, maintained his former air of listlessness & preoccupation, & while his opponent in the game seemed absorbed in study and calculation, carefully guarding her own pieces & taking every advantage over his, he only made an occasional move & that too with scarcely looking at the board. At length she began to complain of his extreme inconsequence, saying that she should win without the excitement of a contest.

"Well," said he, "I'll try to take some interest in the affair just to please your ladyship, but really I feel none."

He now set about trying to defeat her in good earnest. The fortune of the day turned directly, her men were outmaneouvred one after the other, & ere ten minutes had elapsed, she found herself regularly & decisively checkmated. Few tempers are proof to the trial afforded by defeat in a game of chance, & the pouting lip & clouded forehead of the lady showed that hers was not one of the number.

"My dear marchioness of Wellesley," said the earl, "don't take it so much to heart. Try again & I'll be beaten next time."

They were about to recommence the game when my brother came dashing up. "Hah, Aunt," said he, "trying a match with Percy? & by that frown I see you have been vanquished. Well, never mind, come with me & dance off your vexation in a single pas."[45]

"I won't, Arthur," replied the marchioness. "You are eternally teasing me to dance, when you cannot but be aware that the exercise fatigues me to death."

"Nay, dear Aunt, you must not deny me!" replied the persevering Duke, taking her hand with his usual effrontery, in spite of the refusal she had just given him.

"Let me go, mad boy," said she, smiling, however, & struggling but faintly to disengage herself from his grasp.

"I will not, Aunt. You must yield or submit to a fair trial of our respective strengths."

The marchioness now seemed to have found an amusement which suited her, viz., battling with her impetuous & handsome nephew. Nor did she seem anxious to terminate the contest, by either yeilding the point or giving a decided repulse.

Warner, whose interest in her had been entirely removed by the information conveyed in Northangerland's & my brother's modes of addressing her, did not wait to see the issue of the struggle, but turned somewhat discontentedly away with an emphatic "Pshaw".

Continuing his search of a wife, he now directed his attention towards a sofa w[h]ere the Countess of Northangerland was sitting with the duke of Fidena & the Marquis of Marseilles.[46]   The magnet which attracted him there was a young lady whose appearance pleased him more than any he had yet seen.   She was not much above middle size, but looked taller from the slight & stately mould of her figure.   A profusion of pale gold curls shadowed a snow white though not lofty forehead & a set of pretty & open features, rather quiet than animated in themselves, derived all the charms of the most acute & brilliant expression from fine large eyes of the deepest blue.   Her dress was simple: a dark green silk frock, judiciously shortened, discovered a slender ancle & exquisitely formed foot partially covered with a small satin sandal; one string of pearls, large, fair & of the purest water, encircled her neck; & her belt was secured by a superb diamond clasp fastened negligently on one side.   As she stood half sitting, half leaning against the arm of the sofa, Warner could hear her frequently joining in with the conversation of the others which turned on some scientific subject, & from the attention displayed when she spoke, it was evident her opinion was considered of no small value.   Her manner of conversing indeed evinced great knowledge & that too of the recondite order which we do not expect to find in ladies, more especially young ladies, but then her tone, her air, the whole spirit of her words & sentiments was so careless, unconscious, good-humoured, so divested of pretension & so filled with girlish simplicity that all terror of learning was forgotten while listening to her & wondering at her attainments only remained.   Once or twice she was contradicted in some theoretical opinion that she hazarded, by the Duke of Fidena. Immediately she turned to lady Zenobia & appealed to her with a familiarity that few dare use towards that haughty peeress. The countess in directly gave her her support, saying in an apologetical tone to Fidena that she never deserted her pet.

"No," replied the youthful blue,[47] "you do *not*, my noble mistress, & your pet will never desert you, were you to turn alchemist & seek for the philosopher's stone or mechanic & devote yourself to the discovery of the perpetual motion.[48] By the by, my lady, the earl says that if he were me he would not despair of finding out either of those secrets."

"What! My husband?"

"Yes."

"O! nonsense child, he was imposing on your simplicity."

"Not I, Zenobia," said Northangerland, who had been standing for some time unobserved at the back of the sofa. "I really think your clever little favourite might do worse than follow the example of some of your wise philosophers & profound savans who spent their wretched lives in pursuing shadows &, when the delusion finally escaped them, tumbled down to the oblivion of the grave, a mass of as useless & execrable flesh, blood & bones as ever disgraced the form & wasted the abilitites of humanity."

"And should that be my end, my lord?" asked the young lady with a somewhat wistful look at the great nobleman.

"I beg a thousand pardons, madam," he replied, "but I forgot myself, as I often do when talking to ladies. When I only intend raillery & jest, I frequently dart off into earnest & bitterness."

"Then you don't really mean that I should turn either alchemist or mechanic?"

"Why, would not that be as good as linguist & astronomer?"

"Hardly," she replied doubtingly. "Yes, if your lordship thinks — ". Here she suddenly paused. At that moment her eyes fell on M[r]. Warner, & the simple, credulous & uncertain expression of her face gave place to a keen look of curiousity.

"Who is that person?" she asked in an audible whisper.

"Ah, M[r] Warner!" said the Countess of Northangerland, rising & going towards him. "How are you? Ellen, this is M[r] Warner, M[r] Warner, this is Miss Grenville, only daughter of General

Grenville." [49]

"Right enough," said Warner to himself. "I have hit it at last."
He bowed low & expressed his happiness at this new accession
of acquaintance. Ellen did not immediately return his courtesy;
he stood for a few moments looking at him, not at all with the air of
a town-bred lady who scarce knows the meaning of the word astonishment, but with a very positive expression of wonder in her
bright eyes & parted coral lips.

"And is this the celebrated Mr Warner?" were the first words
she spoke.

"It is, indeed," replied the Countess.

"Why," she continued in a tone of disappointment, still gazing
at him, not as if he had been a living man who could hear every
word she uttered but rather as if he were an unconscious picture or
statue, "he is not at all like Zamorna! The Duke told me he was
the image of himself."

Mr Warner's eye began to flash fire. "I am as nature made me,
madam," he said quickly, "& I do not know that I have any reason
either to be ashamed of my own person or to envy that of another."

"Certainly not," replied Miss Grenville now recollecting herself. "Certainly not, Mr Warner Howard Warner Esqr of Warner
hall & Howard Castle. I am happy to see you, Sir, quite happy, &
I trust the great family & its interests prosper."

Warner did not know what to make of this satirical mode of
adressing him. He felt inclined to be very angry, but then the
satirist was so young, so pretty, apparently so goodhumoured &
devoid of malice, that his anger was disarmed before he had time
to express it. He was just about to answer in a corresponding
spirit, when a footman entered & announced that refreshments
were prepared in the refrectory & that the Duchess of Zamorna
now waited the assembling of her guests in that appartment.

"Marshal yourselves," exclaimed the Duke. "Form into rank
& file. Who takes the precedency? I think myself. Zenobia!
Maria! My right & left arms are at your service. Aunt! You, I
know, will go with Northangerland, Fidena will conduct the lady
Edith. Lily! [50] I mean your grace, I see you are already paired
with Jordan. But Ellen, my little blue-bell, who is your choice as
a conductor & a next-neighbour during supper?"

"Yourself, my lord duke."

"Nay, cushat,[51] you see I am doubly engaged, a fair & stately supporter, one royal, the other noble, on each side."

"Then I'll go alone."

"That may hardly be; look around petted child. There's Abercorn, Eagleton, Molyneux, Lascelles, my cousin Fitzroy[52] & a dozen others, all anxious & emulous for the honour of leading you into the supper room."

Ellen smiled & threw a coquestish glance on the throng of young noble-men who vied with each other in offers of their attendance. "Keep off!" said she. "I will have none of you. Mr Warner, for pity's sake, lend me your arm."

In triumph & with a glancing eye, Mr Warner yielded her the required assistance. A few minutes sufficed to get the rest of the cavalcade into due order. All then moved forward toward the supper-room through wide-flung folding doors & uplifted draperies & so, for the present (Exeunt Omnes).[53]

CHAPTER THE IInd

Yet marked I where the bolt of cupid fell:
It fell upon a little azure flower.[54]

Ellen Grenville was, as I have said, the only daughter of General Grenville &, with the exception of two sons, the only child. Her beauty, wit & artlessness had made her his favourite, & the indulgence with which owing to this circumstance she had from her infancy been treated, was the means of rendering her somewhat wilful, careless & capricious. The General's immense wealth is well known; a fourth part of it he had promised to settle on her at his death, consequently she was a heiress. The Countess of Northangerland's instructions & partiality had early entitled her to the appellation of a blue. Fortune, personal attractions & the crowd of suitors which such advantages never fail to draw, occasioned her being not a little of a coquette, & to the almost unlimited supply of money which she had always received was attributable the extravagance which also formed a part of her character. Such is my heroine. The reader will exclaim, "Why, she is little better than a petite maîtresse!"[55] but in justice to Miss Grenville, I must remark that the two most alarming traits, namely Blue & Coquette, were so ameliorated by her native simplicity & good nature as entirely to lose much of what is repulsive & disagreeable in other individuals of the same species. The former character had been imposed on her rather by circumstances than inclination. Lady Zenobia Ellrington, when in the full bloom of woman-hood, had adopted little Ellen Grenville for her pet, her fondling. With her own lips, she had instructed her in the classics, had initiated her into the divine science of astronomy, & had carefully directed her steps in those paths of abstruse Knowledge which she herself delights to tread. Ellen loved her noble preceptress with a devotion which none but the warmhearted, the unsophisticated & the youthful are capable of either feeling or appreciating. She admired, nay almost adored, her. Nor was her affection deficient in those tenderer sympathies which go farther towards creating a firm attachment than all the admiration & cold respect on earth. She had seen Zenobia in her moments of weakness, when love, pride & anguish contended so strongly in her great mind that they well nigh overthrew its equilibrium.[56] She had been the confidant of that unquenchable but most unhappy attachment which Lady Ellrington bore & does still bear towards my brother. Ellen Grenville was ever the third person in their meetings, the companion of their walks, the permitted associate of their mutual studies, the witness of *his* false & insidious & of *her* most sincere & impassioned vows, & finally, she beheld the agony, the intense, deep, racking agony which wrung Zenobia's heart & shook her frame when the intelligence reached her with frighful certainty that he whom she had loved with all the Italian fervour & Roman loftiness of which even her soul was capable,[57] had given his hand, heart, coronet to another. It took time to collect her shattered energies & to dispel the darkness which had fallen round her unrivalled intellect. But happily she did revive & Ellen saw with pleasure the union which her

PLATE 3: Charlotte Brontë, 'King of Angria, Duke of Zamorna', c.1834.
By kind permission of Mrs Eleanore Lang, Canada.

PLATE 4: (*Above*) 'Alexander Percy', Lord Ellrington and Duke of Northangerland, *c*.1833-1834; unfinished watercolour by Charlotte Brontë. By courtesy of the Brontë Society.

PLATE 5: (*Left*) 'Zenobia Marchioness Ellrington', Countess of Northangerland, 15 October 1833; pencil drawing by Charlotte Brontë thought to be copied from a contemporary engraving of the Countess of Blessington. By kind permission of private owner.

patroness soon after formed with the great Percy towards whom, as the kind & attentive husband of Zenobia, the greatest man of his time, the dark, deep, demagogue, subsequently the proud Aristrocrat & the stern upholder of thrones, she experienced a confused amalgamation of feelings in which gratitude, admiration, awe & fear all strangely participated.

About a week after the Grand fête at Wellesley House, Miss Grenville & the Countess of Northangerland were seated alone in the latter's Boudoir. A splendid Terrestrial Globe stood on the table before them & a large folio of maps lay open beside it. The elder lady's thoughful brow & downward gaze of the deepest contemplation indicated that she was engaged in the solution of some intricate Geographical problem. Ellen looked serious likewise, but her thoughts seemed wandering from her ostensible occupation to other & far different subjects. She held a pencil in her fingers & traced listlessly, & apparently unconsciously, figures of hearts, Cupids, true love knots & other amatory emblems on the margins of the costly atlas.[58] At last the Countess noticed her abstraction; she looked up.

"Ellen," said she, "what are you doing, child? Zamorna challenged me to solve this problem in half an hour & I have already been poring twenty minutes over it. Make haste & help me!"

"I can't, my lady."

"& why not? What are you thinking about?"

"About my lovers. They are so many, I really don't know what to do with them."

"Turn them off, child!"

"Aye & break their hearts, poor things. No, I am not so cruel as that. They would all die of consumptions & then I should be blamed for killing them."

"Nonsense! They would go fluttering after some other butterfly, & quite forget the one they had formerly pursued. It is the way of men, Ellen. They have not hearts like us," & the countess sighed deeply.

"Now don't get sad, mistress," said Ellen. "Don't begin to think of the Duke. I believe his eyes, his curls, his lips, his form, his very fingers, long, slim, deceitful-looking emblems of himself as they are, are impressed in your heart with a stamp whose mark is ineffaceable."

"Your belief is but too well founded, child. I can never forget him! Never! Never! But I have one consolation: I am not the only sufferer by him; others have felt the same agonies as myself. Two have died from his neglect."[59]

"O that Zamorna! I could hate him, my lady, but when I see him it is impossible. His voice is so soft & sweet, his manner to you is so cordial, so frank & bland & brotherly."

"Silence, child! It is not brotherly! I am not his Sister! I never will be his sister! I have no sisterly affection for him! Don't mention the word brother to me again. I tell you, child, I love him and always shall love him. I don't care how he has scorned, deceived, rejected me. There is a charm, a talisman about him which wins all hearts & rivets chains round them which can never be undone."

"My lady," said Miss Grenville with an alarmed look, "remember Northangerland."

"I do remember Northangerland & that maddens me. I admire Alexander; I am proud of him, nay, I adore him. But oh, Ellen, Ellen, a first love cannot be washed away! The image of that boy with his falcon eyes & bright hair & fascinating voice, whose sound was as sweet as honey dew, will haunt me to my dying hour. I sometimes think it will drive me mad!"

"Forget it, my lady, at least for a time. Come, you shall put away these Globes, the problem will remind you of him. Shut up that Atlas, there are his pencil marks on this Angrian map. Remove all books, every one of them have been in his hand & must have his name written in them. Nay, let alone that locket, for you are always looking at it & the miniature is so infernally like him I wish it was burnt. Turn now to the picture of Percy: the face is as handsome, the form is as noble. There, that is right. Smile at it, it smiles at you. Now, my lady, you love Alexander better than all the world beside. You hate the imperial Deceiver & so do I, & shall continue to do so till — "

"Till when, Ellen?" interrupted the Countess. "Aye, till the next time he smiles & calls you his blue-bell & reads Homer with you in tones that might make High Dutch sound melodious. Will the hatred last longer, think you, child?"

"Perhaps not, but meantime I do really dislike him just now & therefore let us talk no more of him, mistress. I want your advice about my own lovers. Papa says he shall insist on my making a choice of one of them before long, & mamma is always teasing me on the subject of a settlement for life. Now hearken to the tale of those who are at present on my list in the capacity of declared suitors & tell me which you think most eligible."

With these words Miss Grenville produced a little memorandum book bound in silk & clasped with silver. She opened it & read from its pages the following entries: "Lord Abercorn, held in temporary abeyance for pastime. Honourable William Lascelles ditto. Lord Alexander Musselburg ditto. Captain Julian Gordon[60] rejected. Arthur O'Connor Esq[61] ditto; returned to the charge but was again blackballed. Sir Robert Pelham, Baronet, was every thing that could be desired in fortune, person, manners, standing, but I could not stoop to accept what another lady had declined, so wrote his name on the oyster shell likewise.[62] Lord Macara Lofty, under consideration. Warner Howard Warner Esq[r] under *deep* consideration. Those are all the present train whose happiness for life is in my hands. On which head shall I place the crown of election?"

"Stop, Ellen! How lightly you speak! Did you say Viscount Lofty was among the number of your suitors?"

"Yes."

"And do you like him?"

"Hem, I can hardly tell. At first I detested him most cordially, or rather I felt afraid of him. He has such strange eyes, so sly & dangerous & with an obliquity of vision that is absolutely startling, but after a while I became accustomed to that peculiarity, & his persuasive tongue, high bred manners & cultivated mind made me half inclined to give him the preference. Besides both Papa & mamma evidently favoured him, & perhaps by this time I should have been Viscountess Lofty, had it not been for the appearance of M[r] Warner. Now, to speak truth, I believe I really love that extraordinary man! In the beginning, I almost despised him. He is so womanish in outward form, with little, silly, white hands & a smooth beardless chin, but he has eyes like living diamonds, a brow of the true intellectual fashion, a mind as gigantic & masculine as his body is slight & effeminate. All his actions, every word he speaks, every sentence that falls from his tongue are characterized by an energy that astonishes the more by its contrast with his corporeal fragility. Faults he has, to be sure, & at them I have laughed & sneered till sheer terror compelled me to be silent. Last night when I was satirizing him, he breathed so hard & flashed such blighting brilliancy from his eyes that I positively paused in the midst of a sentence & condescended to beg pardon for my impertinence."

"Did you, Ellen? Well, you must be far gone indeed if you stooped to that! But since Warner has obtained such strong possession of your heart, why don't you at once give him your hand?"

"Because I dare not. Papa has half promised me to Lofty & you know that his spoken word goes as far as most other men's written oaths. I know that if I were to make a stand he would yield to me because I am his pet, but then I should wish, if possible, to have his free, full & unsolicited consent to my union when I do marry, otherwise the light yoke of matrimony might in judgement turn to a heavy burden."

"Right, Ellen, you have a sensible head though a merry heart, child. Be ruled by circumstances, but don't go against the General. Listen, there is the dinner bell. We have a small, select party at Ellrington House to-day. Zamorna is one of the Guests. Can you make good your promise of hating him?"

"I'll try. Now you shall see, my lady, whether I have not resolution for anything. It shall be my part to set you an example of stern antipathy to vice, however fair the form in which it may be enshrined."

When the ladies reached the dining-room they found that the company were already seated. The Earl of Northangerland, of course, presided. My brother sat on his right hand & near him the Honourable Miss Montmorency. Opposite were the Duchess & Mr Montmorency; Lady Percy,[63] General Thornton, Mr Warner & Mr Babbicombe Morley[64] & myself formed the rest of the party. It was, in fact, a coterie of the great leaders of the Angrian faction. Zenobia's seat was left vacant for her &, after bowing to her Guests, she advanced to take it with a some what discontented book, for it happened that Thornton had been marshalled out as her next neighbour & with that worthy personage she has few ideas in common because, though the General is both a nobleman & a gentleman (Injustice has deprived him nominally of the first mentioned rank but it was out of its power to render the deprivation more than nominal)[65] yet he has too much of my father in him, too little of my brother to be at all agreeable to her. Dinner passed over with the discussion of only General topics. Northangerland & Montmorency chiefly upheld the conversation, for Warner was engaged with Miss Grenville, Babbicome Morley in paying due attention to the costly edibles which courted him on all sides, & Zamorna seemed to have taken a fit of unusual taciturnity, his principal employment being fixed & placid contemplation of the Countess, who sat in a desperate ill humour, austerely declining all the attempts which Thornton politely made to entertain her. But though the feast of reason & the flow of soul[66] was nearly entirely confined to the two great men I have mentioned, to the daughters of both & the mother of the first, yet they furnished it in no grudging or stinted measure.

By the bye, few sights afford me greater or more elevated pleasure than the spectacle of Northangerland presiding in a social circle: that man, whose fortunes have been so strange, so wild, so wonderful, whose character is so steeped in outer darkness; the parricide, the pirate, the land-robber, the rebel, the insolvent; to see him surounded by the fair & noble, himself the stateliest, the most perfectly aristocratic amongst them; to view the subdued, graceful refinement of his manner, his lofty politeness mingled with the slightest possible dash of the precision of the old school, & well does that court-bred precision sit on him. It becomes his tall slender form, his high & commanding forehead, his dress of grave yet rich simplicity. But it contrasts strangely with his known character, his sneering & sarcastic expression of countenance, his treacherous eye & the wild expletives; the horrifying piratical oaths which now & then drop from his lips in tones as soft as the words are tremendous. How different is all this from Arthur's bold & daring Gallantry: his bearing so fraught with military hauteur, his impassioned bursts of feeling, generally of an angry or scornful nature, in the revelation of which eye, voice, cheek, form & forehead seem all animated, all eloquent with the same overwhelming & outflashing spirit. Northangerland invariably displays the greatest deference towards ladies. Zamorna, in that respect, is about on a par with the Grand Sultan of Turkey surrounded by his Seraglio:[67] he humours them, understands every avenue to their hearts, possesses universal influence amongst them, but he pays them no deference. I rather believe that, in his secret heart of hearts, a casket which none have ever unlocked save himself, he thinks them far inferior to the lords of Creation & imagines that they were created only to furnish him with amusement & to do his pleasure. Zenobia! Julia! Maria! Henrietta! Is not the doctrine of this creed a pestilent heresy? Yet your idol professes, cherishes & acts upon it.

After dinner the ladies adjourned to the drawing room; I accompanied them. Coffee was handed round in a service of the costliest china, & while we sipped that refreshing beverage, a few topics of gossip & scandal were introduced in order to wile away the time. Every one seemed to relish this piquant ingredient in their coffee cups, from the haughty Zenobia to the goodnatured Ellen. Even Mary, whose fine mind & exquisite delicacy of taste might, one would suppose, have induced her to reject such conversation as not sufficiently refined, kindled into interest while she listened, and her bright hazel eyes absolutely gleamed with the light of satire as at one time, with a few sharply severe words, she herself touched off the character of lady Sydney, glanced at that of the princess Maria, & with the lightness & keeness of a frost wind in winter even skimmed over the foibles of her present stepmother. A little while afterwards, when we were sitting alone in a window recess, I asked her if she was not slightly inclined to be jealous.

"I have no cause," answered she quickly. "Adrian knows I am better than all my rivals & he loves me ten times more. He does not love them, not one of them; he told me so himself & said mine was the only head that should ever be encircled by his Coronet, were it Ducal, Royal or Imperial!"

"And you trust him?" I asked.

"I cannot do otherwise," she replied. "No, Charles, it is a moral impossibility to doubt Zamorna. When you hear him speak, he is so truthful, noble & honourable, the kingly & patrician blood that rushes through his veins will not let him lie. Wellington never was false; Arthur cannot be so. The Poet who surpassed Byron, the warrior who equalled my father, the hero who counted life as lighter than dust when weighted in the balance with glory — he to turn a deceiver? No, never, never! Charles, I tell you that Zamorna, with all that is great & bright about him, is mine & mine only!"

How she looked at that moment! Divinely lovely! I said nothing, for I could not weaken her enthusiastic confidence, but a sigh escaped me to think that it might have the sand, instead of the rock, for its foundation. And now the unfolded doors admitted the party from the dining-room. As they entered, Miss Mortmorency was performing with brilliant effect on the piano-forte; most of them gathered round her to listen. There were, however, two exceptions: her father & my brother. The former planted himself on the hearth-rug with his back to the fire & looked with some contempt towards the group whose attention was absorbed by the music. The latter advanced to our recess. He unceremoniously compelled me to evacuate the seat I occupied besides Mary &, establishing his own sublime person there in my stead, began to converse with her.

"Hah, Henrietta," said he, "what were you thinking about when I entered the room? By the brilliance of that eye & cheek I should guess it was something very exciting."

"No less so than yourself, Adrian," she replied with a smile.

"Indeed! Well, Mary, to speak truth I never think of you when we are separate."

"Don't you, Arthur?" she said, & her sweet eyes looked up in his face with an expression of sudden sadness.

"No, love, because I never see anything fair enough to remind me of you."

Mary drew closer towards him, leaned her forehead against his shoulder for a minute, & then, again looking up, said with a sigh, "Arthur, I fear there will be nothing like you in heaven."

"Dearest," he replied, "If the Angels that meet you after Death are like me, be on your Guard lest they should prove fallen angels: would not trust the heaven whose spirits were of mould so mortal.

God knows I am no inhabitant for regions of sanctification. That must be a fiery ordeal which should fit me for communion with martyred saints and the souls of unjust men made perfect."

"But Arthur, I could have no sympathy with beings brighter or more glorious than you; I might dread, perhaps admire, but not love them."

"Don't fear that you will ever be put to the proof," said the voice of Northangerland, who had joined them unobserved. "The Grave, Corruption, Annihilation, are the only followers of Death. Mary, you see in Zamorna & myself the perfection of created things. Man is the master-piece of nature, or of him who commanded the existence of nature. We are formed both mentally & corporeally in the first mould of humanity. Look then, look earnestly, look long. No fairer, no nobler spectacle will ever be presented to your gaze. Dreamers think otherwise but I say "the first dark day of nothingness"[68] comes after the heart is still & the eye glazed forever." Northangerland uttered these words in a low tone, solemnly & without much of the cold sarcasm that usually chills & withers whatever falls from his lips. There was an awful sterness on his dark, bent brow & in his eye, whose concentrated light seemed as if it would pierce to his daughter's heart while he spoke to her. Mary trembled but showed no other sign either of fear, surprise, or sorrow.

Zamorna muttered, "great dangerous Infidel", & strode away with a countenenace as black as night. The cloud had cleared up, however, & given place to his usual deceitful smile by the time he reached the opposite end of the room, where the Countess of Northangerland & Miss Grenville were sitting. The latter bridled up as he approached & endeavoured to assume an air of coldness & reserve.

"Well," said he, taking her hand with as much cool effrontery as can well be imagined, "how blows my flower to day? Its bell droops, I think. Ah! I had forgot, it is evening, & the leaves must close! What shrinking! Turning its blossom from the sun! Now that, lord but bless me! Caprice in a flower! Zenobia, what on earth ails my blue-bell?"

The Countess smiled. "She is trying to hate you," replied she. "If she succeeds, her resolution will be stronger than mine."

A slight sneer curled the Duke's short Grecian upper lip. "Hate me?" said he. "Aye, let her if she can, freakish, spoiled, petted baby. I defy her to hate me one instant!" He folded his arms & stood over Ellen, gazing at her most intently with an expression that strongly tempted Warner, who sat at no great distance, to pistol him on the spot. The farce could not last long. Ellen began to giggle; she attempted to rise but the Duke prevented her.

"Sit there," said he, "till you feel inclined to recant."

She hid her face, fidgeted, blushed, tittered, & at length, unable to hold out any longer, she turned to Zenobia & said, "Misstress, I'll hate him some other day, but just now I can't for my life!"

A general laugh followed this naïve confession. Warner alone did not join in it. He felt angry & it was sometime before he could dismiss the unpleasant feelings that harrassed him. At length, however, he in some measure succeeded in mastering that irritability which is his besetting sin. He then rose & walked towards lady Northangerland's sofa. The Duke was now seated between her & Ellen. Lady Percy occupied an arm chair near her noble son & her fair grandaughter stood behind it, & gathered round were Montmorency, Thornton, Morley, &c., listening to Zamorna, who was speaking with rapid & animated emphasis.

"Our influence," said he, "that is my own & my father in law's, is unbounded. It pervades all ranks, circles, grades & degrees of society. We can introduce happiness or misery, peace or dissension alike into a private family or a public council. The power is great, even sublime, &, by heaven, I would share it with none if I could help it; but that Great, vile, splendid, hateful, fiendish, angelic, black, bright, abominable, blessed scoundrel, that Northangerland, that illustriously infamous relative of mine, whom I abhor & yet admire, detest & yet love, that bundle of contradictions & yet that horribly consistent whole — he forsooth will share in the power & I cannot hinder him."

"Be cool, Arthur," interrupted Northangerland, laughing at his son-in law's vehemence. "Don't work yourself up into an artificial passion. Do you hear me rage against your royal self in that style? Yet have I not as much cause? Nay" (glancing keenly towards the Countess) "have I not more?"

The Duke made no answer. There was a pause which was broken by Thornton. "Yes, my lords," said he, "you are the two great Drivers of Verdopolis, that is certain: it goes as you lead, & I expect your influence will be shown over the higher spheres at least when you take your intended trip to Wellington's land." [69]

"Aye," said Montmorency, "there will be whole squares of great houses standing with the blinds down, shutters closed, knockers silent. Ebor Terrace, Grenville Street & the other fashionable thoroughfares will have some rest from the roll of carriages. I think I, for one, shall take a trip to the Green Country. Julia, you remember Derrinane." [70]

"Yes, father, though I have not seen it since I was seven years old. Will Harriette & Frederic [71] go with us?"

"No," interrupted Zamorna. "I have already secured lord & lady Castlereagh for my party, & now I invite all here present. Zenobia, you, of course, are one of ourselves, so are you — mamma (to lady Percy). "Thornton, you will go though Fidena, his Duchess, my bright Maria & the Princess Royal should accompany you." [72]

"Aye, to be sure," replied the General. "I'm not so crabbed as they are: it's all one to me whether I be with them or better folk."

"That's right, Thornton, ever hearty my lad! Now, Morley, will you go?"

"Why, your Grace is aware that there are two things to be considered: public weal & private gratification. I should not hesitate to sacrifice the first to the last for the space of a few weeks, were there not like wise two other things to be considered, pleasure & profit. In case I accepted your Grace's invitation, I should have to employ an under secretary to fulfil the duties of my office. That would by no means advantage me; therefore I am under the disagreeable necessity of returning a negative answer."

"You might have done so in fewer words, sir. Now, Bluebell, can you bear to accompany so odious a person as myself?"

"Perhaps not. But I shall have great pleasure in accompanying the earl & Countess."

"Humph. Warner, you must go to watch the game. The Lofty Hawks will be there."

Warner bowed acquiescence. Northangerland now took out his gold repeater. He struck it. "It is ten o'clock," said he. "I move that we all adjourn to the opera. Arthur, their will be more opportunities for making verbal invitations. Allons,[73] as poor Bernadotte[74] would say." The motion was unanimously agreed to. Carriages & servants were called & thus I drop the curtain.

CHAPTER THE IIIrd

A change comes o'er the spirit of
our dream[75]

When la voile du thèatre[76] is raised again, our readers must picture to them selves, not the streets, squares, terraces & alleys of Verdopolis, with its presiding dome, pacific harbour, busy quay & that human tide which never ebbs inundating all its thoroughfares, but the peaceful scences of Wellington's land as they have been inimitably described by Sir John Flower.[77] I need not relate the wonders of that journey, or rather progress, which embraced in its course every thing noble in Africa. The public prints for weeks past have teemed with accounts of the aggregate splendour which the efforts of our aristocracy produced when the head of each noble family vied with his equals & superiors in the attempt to produce unsurpassed magnificence and all fell short of the princely profusion, the regal state, maintained with such proud consistency by the great Leaders & originators of the journey — Northangerland & his royal son-in law.

The hearts of my father's subjects were rejoiced: there was a holiday, a general festival throughout the land wherever the bright train passed, & the meanest peasant in the lowest hut toasted the health of his future queen, the lovely Mary Henrietta, in the jug not of muddy ale but of rich red wine with which her bounty had furnished him. I travelled in my brother's cortège & consequently had frequent opportunities of being a close observer of the Duchess during the journey. At every town, village & hamlet which we passed, addresses were presented & crowds gathered to welcome the bride of Zamorna. Her popularity was enhanced by the circumstance of her being a native of the country & because she owed existence to the tremendous, the dreaded Northangerland. Never have I seen any thing so fascinating as the sweet yet noble condescension of her manner. She would descend from her carriage & advance unattended into a throng of bold & hardy peasantry, gliding through their stern rough ranks like a sunbeam & answering their hoarse thunders of congratulation that shook the very welkin,[78] in tones so sweet, so soft, in words so prompt & appropriate & in a manner so totally unembarrassed, so queenly yet so feminine & gentle, that her rude auditors, unable to resist the charm of her speech & appearance, would frequently burst into a simultaneous prayer for all the blessings of heaven above & of the deep that lieth under to be showered on the lovely angel who was imparadised in such sweet flesh. Yet, notwithstanding this intoxicating reception, she was never once tempted by flattery, by the impulse of the moment or by the desire of popularity, to utter one imprudent sentence, to forget for one instant the dignity of the rank she occupied. Mary knew well the character of her future subjects. She remembered her own proud, fastidious, haughty lord who ever watched her with eyes so keen & jealous: she knew that graceful confidence was what he wished, what he would reward by smiles & carresses that to her were priceless, but that anything approaching to familiarity would be instantly followed by the averted countenance, by that cold air of neglect whose calm & silent displeasure was worse than the hottest anger which gives itself vent in words. As an instance of the aristocratic exclusiveness which in spite of her mildness & condescension she still maintained, I may remark that she never once shook hands with another or even permitted her own hand to be kissed except once, & that was when the mayor of a Town asked it as a boon in the name of the whole corporation. Even then a glove covered her slender fingers & shortly after, when the Duke called her to his side, I saw her quietly replace it with another pair which one of her waiting-maids handed her.

Percy-Hall is the scene to which I have now transported my readers, as it formed the first resting-place of the splendid cavalcade which accompanied its awful owner. A lovely Spring morning dawned on the first day after our arrival there, & I rose early to enjoy a walk before breakfast on the sweet lawns which were spread beneath my chamber window. The picture of the splendid & venerable pile of buildings that constitute the hall, the slopes of sunny verdure that surround it, the noble trees, principally elms of the grandest dimensions, that cover those slopes with trembling gloom, interlaced by continual bursts of light, must be imprinted in the heart of every one who has read *The Politics of Verdopolis*[79] — & who has not?

A thousand thoughts, some sweet, some solemn, crowded into my mind, as I slowly wandered through that classic scenery & mused on *his* life & character to whom everything around me belonged. I now beheld the landscape in perfection. Dew & sunrise lit the greensward till it glistened like a floor of emeralds. All the Elm Trees threw their mighty morning shadows westward & such wild flowers as grew round their trunks & roots were saturated with the moisture that the breeze & the early birds showered from their wet boughs & foliage. A cloudless sky, a warm, balmy atmosphere, the expansive park, whose verdure was impearled with the dew that covered it, an horizon of blue, misty hills & a nearer prospect of many groups of deer, completed the magnificient panorama now presented to my eyes. Could this be a scene for crime, could the lordly mansion which, with its porticos, its long, low casements, its many gables all grey & time honoured, & its picturesque stacks of chimneys, formed the central object of the scene: could it, I say, have given rendezvous to traitors, to robbers, to outlaws? I dared not answer my self in the affirmative, yet so it was. & if the dark & appalling rumour may be credited, the walls of that haughty house have once echoed the dying moans of a father murdered, if not by the hands yet at the instigation of his own son.[80] Yes they now harbour a parricide. But let us not remember these things. If the dark deed was ever done, the lapse of twenty years has since clouded it in impenetrable obscurity. Retribution may arrive, when or how it is not for man to say, but the instrument[81] still exists who was employed to perpetrate what a higher power had devised, his feet yet make haste to shed blood & "Justice" we are told "commends the poisoned chalice &c."[82]

Reflections such as these occupied my mind as I paced quietly through the green glades of the chase. They were agreeably dissipated & happier thoughts substituted in their place by the unexpected apparition of Flower's lovely heroine. There she glided before me, through the changing lights & shadows of a long plane tree avenue. As simple, as elegant, as fair, as unsophisticated as when, with Byron's poems in her hand, she first met Sir Robert Pelham & commenced that acquaintance which had nearly terminated in matrimony. The Duchess of Zamorna & the Queen of Angria is the same flower of nature whose beauties have been enhanced, though hardly changed, by cultivation as was Mary Henrietta Percy. She was quite alone, not even Roland[83] followed her fairy steps over the green glittering grass, & beneath the waving foliage that every where carpet & overhang the noble pleasure-grounds of Percy Hall.

I ran up to her. "Good morning, Mary, you have risen with the Lark I think. How long have you been up?"

"Half an hour, not more. A skylark waked me as it flew by my chamber window & I could neither resist its song nor the cool sweet air that blew over me as I opened the lattice. Not a soul except the servants is stirring in the house beside you & I. I listened at every door as I passed through the corridor & there is neither voice nor speech heard among them."

"Lazy loiterers!" was my reply. "They don't know what they are losing by preferring their hot beds to this delicious sunrise. But come, Mary, we'll make the most of our time. What say you to a chase in the park? I'll try to catch you before you reach that European white poplar surrounded by paling."

It required but small entreaty to induce Mary to fall in with my proposal. She hardly ever denies me anything & the young patrician beauty who is so cold & proud to her equals, or those that think themselves so, with me throws of[f] her assumed haughtiness & reveals all her natural gaiety & animation. Flinging her hat on to the grass in order to be more at liberty, she started off at once like a roe. I strove in vain to reach her; she flew as lightly as a lapwing. Scarcely touching the poplar which was to have been her goal, she bounded away in the track of a deer that her rustling dress, rather than her noiseless step, had startled. One group of antlered browzers took the alarm after another. I now helped to rouse them & soon fawns, hinds & harts were scouring the park in all directions, through tangled alleys & open glades, to the infinite amusement of myself & my fair companion. In the very height of our pastime we were suddenly checked by seeing a group of gentlemen advancing down the carriage road from the hall.

Mary paused. "Now who are those," said she in a tone of vexation, but not of confusion, "that are coming to interrupt our chase? Ha, I see, my father [and] Montmorency. Look, he is winking at me with the most familiar air imaginable! He thinks I shall be prodigiously ashamed, I dare say! Sir Robert Pelham, absolutely attempting to smile; the Duke of Fidena, grave & serene; & General Thornton — laughing outright. Well, I can bear them all! Charles, give me your hand. Let us go to meet them; my father beckons."

Quietly & slowly the youthful Duchess advanced towards where the imposing group above describe[d] were standing. Her head uncovered, her bright hair waving in a hundred wild curls over her brow & temples, her eyes full of sparkling life & her complexion, usually more remarkable for its delicacy than brilliancy, heightend to a tint of the richest & softest crimson. Northangerland held out his hand to her as she approached.

"Good morning, child," said he, shaking his head but smiling at the same time. "After the deer as usual, I see, without bonnet, regardless of the wet grass. Mary, you are as much a child as ever!"

"How does the scent lie this morning, my lady?" asked Montmorency with a leer.

"I don't know, Mʳ Montmorency," she replied simply & with the perfect air of her great father when he chuses to take anything literally which is intended as a jest.

"I think," said Sir Robert, "it would be dangerous to hunt in company with your Grace."

"Would it, sir?" answered Mary.

"Yes, because the pursuit might turn from the legitimate game to the fair Diana[84] of the hunting party, & the graceful & birdlike speed which she has displayed this morning assures me every attempt at overtaking her would be vain."

"Yes, for you, Pelham," said Montmorency. "She might slacken step, you know, for those she thought worthy of her company. Now if the Duke — "

"Mr Montmorency," said Mary.

"Enough of this, Gentlemen," remarked the Earl sternly. "We will now return to the house, where I believe most of my guests are waiting breakfast for us." Fidena offered Henrietta his arm, observing that she might be fatigued with her morning's exercise.

"Nay, my lord," replied she, without any of the laconic reserve which had marked her behaviour to the others. "Did I run as if I were weary?"

"My lady," said Thornton, offering her his arm on the other side, which action brought an additional shade of gravity over the countenance of Fidena, "you ran as swift as the wind. I never saw either hare or deer go swifter! But can you ride on horseback as well? If so, the pleasures of the chase are at your command any day, & I wish you would avail your self of them. Ladies used to hunt formerly."

Mary laughed. "My dear General, I have no taste for the pleasures of the chase, but I *can* ride on horseback — how well, you shall have an opportunity of judging after breakfast, when it is my intention to propose a ride to the whole party. Such a lovely day as this must not be suffered to pass unimproved."

"Has your Grace marked out any particular direction in which to go?" asked Pelham.

"No, Sir Robert, can you furnish me with a hint on that head?"

"I can. That is, provided your noble father & the duke of Zamorna should not disapprove of the suggestion, it would give me great pleasure to entertain yourself & your Guests at Tamworth Hall to-day. Am I asking too great a favour?"

"O no! Certainly not, provided I can obtain the concurrence of those whom you mention. Father, will you go?"

"I don't mind. Yes, if it will please you, child."

PLATE 6: 'Portrait of A French Brunette', 14 May 1833; watercolour by Charlotte Brontë reminiscent of her early heroines like Ellen Grenville. By courtesy of the Brontë Society.

PLATE 7: 'Bessy Bell and Mary Gray', 15 December 1830; watercolour copy of an engraving by William Finden in the annual *Forget Me Not*, a gift book for 1831. By courtesy of the Brontë Society.

This was all the reply the Earl deigned to bestow; no acknowledgment, no thanks to Sir Robert, but merely a cold acquiescence to please his darling daughter. They now reached the house. Long windows opening like glass doors on to the lawn admitted them into the breakfast room. It was filled with brilliant forms, either walking together in groups or sitting in clusters on the various sofas & ottomans. Mary's glance passed over all to find her adored husband whom she had not seen for the day. She soon perceived him, standing near an open casement, the fascinating & beautiful Maria Sneachi hanging on his arm, & Zenobia, to whom he was speaking, sitting near. Maria's eyes, black as jet & bright as diamonds, were fixed earnestly & almost tenderly on the Duke's noble features, her coral lips were parted & she seemed to be drinking in with eagerness every word he uttered. The sight could not be pleasing to Henrietta, yet she would have gazed long at it, unmindful of the bitter & sick feeling which — inspite of herself — it occasioned at her heart, had not Northangerland somewhat abruptly accosted her:

"Look another way, child," said he, "that spectacle can have no charms for you. The fiend is incurable, hang him! I wish our ladies would cease to offer the incense with which they are continually feeding his insatiable vanity. Look, now, at that Princess: handsome fool, she is on the high-road to misery & perhaps death, if ever woman was."

With a deadly scowl the Earl turned away & so did his daughter; both retired to a distant recess where they could not see what was naturally so displeasing to them. Breakfast was now handed round on silver salvers by a train of liveried attendants. While that meal was in progress Sir Robert Pelham again brought forward his proposal of an excursion to Tamworth Hall. It was received with the cordial consent of the company. Mary listened if she could hear the voice of the Duke amongst the variety of tones that murmured round her, but the well known sound was unheard &, rising from her seat, she stepped forward to see if he still occupied his former station. He was not there, & through the window she could perceive him on the lawn at a little distance, half-reclined on a garden chair which was placed beneath the shadow of a tall elm. Lady Maria sat beside him & was at that moment handing him his coffee from a small ebony stand that had been brought out on to the lawn. He positively looked like a young Persian Satrap[85] submissively attended by a beautiful & favourite slave. Mary compressed her lips firmly as she looked at him. She turned to her father.

"Go to the heartless, arrogant, noble scoundrel yourself," said he.

"I dare not," she replied.

"Mary! Dare not? Are you my daughter?"

"& must I ask his permission to go to Tamworth Hall, to the house of Sir Robert Pelham?"

"You must."

She said no more. Northangerland had uttered those words decisively & it was not for her to disobey him. With a fluttering heart, but a firm tread, she stepped over the window & glided across the lawn. Some fragments of their conversation were audible as she approached them. The haughty, proud Maria — for in spite of her gaiety & sprightliness she is haughty — was now fanning the recumbent nobleman to keep off the flies that had been called to life by the warm summer like morning air.

"Noble Ilderim,"[86] said she as, with the grace & state proper to her royal rank, she performed this menial office, "our prophet's proudest descendant, do you not think that the west wind now blowing towards us is like

> The light wings of Zephyr oppressed with perfume
> That sigh through the Gardens of Gul in their bloom?[87]

"Light of my eyes," replied the Duke, "my lovely Zulma,[88] the breath of this wind is sweet, but not like that which sweeps over the rose gardens of Suristan.[89] Life, not luxury, is the burden borne on this wind; vigour not voluptuousness. I have been in Persia & felt that

> The gale that breathed from that blue sky,
> The wind to Earth that fell,
> Had magic in its softest sigh
> And in its lightest swell;

And every breath that wandered by
And whispered still felicity
Came o'er me like a spell.

From morn till the decay of light,
I could have sat alone
And watched through all the silent night
To listen to its tone;
For sweetest when the moon was bright
And stars rose dancing on the sight
Fell down that dying moan.

But Maria, I hear a step, who comes this way? Tell me, my
repose is too luxurious to be disturbed. Ilderim has overcome
Zamorna & I am just now little better than a Mahometan lounger
in good earnest."

Before the Princess could answer, Mary was at the Duke's side.
She quietly wrested the fan from her rival's hand.

"Lady Maria," said she, "I can attend my husband. Will you
suffer me to have a few minutes' conversation with him in
private?"

At this moment the trio presented a most unique spectacle.
Arthur perfectly unmoved, his eye even lit by a faint smile of
triumph; Mary pale as death with anger, but calm, as the strictest
good-breeding & politeness could desire; & Maria standing opposite, her tall figure drawn up to its full height and her cheek, brow,
neck & temples all flushed & glowing like a rose. Soon, without
speaking, she dropped a profound courtsey & sailed haughtily
away. My brother broke out into a suppressed laugh. He started
from his recumbent posture & bounded after her as rapidly &
lightly as a mountain wild-deer. The hanging foliage of the alley
down which both were gone soon hid him from Mary's aching
sight. She stood for some minutes like a statue. This vile &
unprovoked neglect cut her to the very heart. Passionate tears
started into her eyes; the blood came back indignantly to her
marble white face; &, trembling with agitation, she was obliged to
sink for support onto the seat her false lord had just vacated.

"I have only been married three months," were the words that broke unconsciously from her lips, "& this is to be my treatment. But my father shall know of it! Be the consequences what they will, I cannot, will not & ought not to bear it.! O Zamorna, you don't care now what anguish you cause me. It used to be different!"

She did not long remain alone. The Duke of Fidena & the Earl of Northangerland soon appeared, coming towards her from opposite directions.

"Madam," said the former in a tone of great kindness & sympathy, "I fear you have suffered some vexation. Is my sister the cause?"

Mary's fast falling tears were a sufficient reply.

"Child," asked Northangerland very sternly, "is he gone without speaking to you?"

"He is," she whispered. "But, father, don't be angry."

Unmindful of her appealing look he gloomily knit his brows & muttered, "Now, by the bones of Sylla,[90] this must be ammended."

"By all that's sacred, it must & that speedily," responded Fidena with equal decision of tone & manner.

"Solomon[91] & his duplicate — a pair of sententious asses," said the well known voice of Zamorna, & the magnificent scoundrel sprang at that instant over the back of the garden chair, & seating himself by his weeping wife, he drew her unresisting hand under his. "What is the occasion of all this weeping & gravity?" he asked, regarding both the offended noblemen as coolly & brazenly as possible.

"Your conduct, Arthur," replied Fidena.

"My conduct? What? I suppose you are offended, John, because a King & princess were so undignified as to run each other a race down the avenue. It was rather out of character, I confess, but you must remember that we are now on our royal progress of relaxation from the cares of state, & besides, the slip in dignity was more than compensated for by the good work it has accomplished. Maria was in danger of losing her good humour, as Mary knows, & I have now fully restored it."

It was vain to talk to so hardened a sinner, & Fidena & Northangerland, both striving to suppress a smile at his easy nonchalance, moved away half-angry & half-amused, leaving Mary to make it up with him as she could.

Before speaking to her, he continued for some time to sit playing with her fingers & lightly passing his hand through her abundant & clustering ringlets. Erelong she ceased to sob, the tears that had fallen so sadly & plentifully down her fair cheeks were wiped away, a serene smile gleamed in her dewy eyes & it broke out into full sunshine when he at last addressed [her] in his usual inexpressible tones.

"Well," said he, "I won't ask the reason why all this waste of tears & sighs is incurred because I can half guess. Never mind! Woman's grief is neither deep nor lasting; the cause & the effect are generally about equally trivial. So cheer up, Mary, & tell me what you had to say to me when you gave Maria such an unequivocal hint that her company was not desired just now."

"Dear Arthur, I had only to ask — to ask — in short, I wished to know whether you would approve of my being one of a party who are about to take a ride to Tamworth Hall this morning?"

"What, with Sir Robert Pelham, I presume?"

"Yes. But now, my lord, don't be displeased with me. Don't draw your hand away; I will not let it go. Can you think that Sir Robert Pelham is more in my eyes than the dirt on which I tread? Adrian, I have no wish to accompany him. It was only in obedience to my father's express command that I ventured to trouble you on the subject at all. You have only to say the word, shall I go or stay?"

It was some moments ere the Duke answered her question. He then said, rising from his seat at the same time, "You may go, Henrietta. My political interests require me to keep up appearances with Sir Robert because he is one of the heads of that moderate party in parliament whose services during late transactions have frequently been invaluable to me. Therefore, there would be little wisdom in disobliging him in so trifling an affair as the present."

"And shall we have your company, my lord? Say yes, then the pleasure will be perfect."

"For about ten miles you will, no further. Now go, love, & prepare for the excursion. I will give orders to the servants & acquaint the rest of the company with our determination."

He then moved away & Mary slowly walked up towards the hall. It was noon before all the company were assembled in the great court yard behind the house. I never saw a more striking spectacle. Upwards of two hundred prancing steeds, each held by a groom splendidly attired, Gentlemen & noblemen in their sumptuous array, ladies in their plumes & long, sweeping saddle-cloths of velvet, the neighing of the horses, the clattering of their iron hoofs on the flagged pavement, the joyous animation of all around, the cloudless sky, the brilliant sunlight, the fresh wind, the great Trees waving & swaying about on each side of the broad smooth road visible through the open gates of the yard, & the handsome & picturesque offices built all round completed a scene such as has few parallels in life.

My attention was chiefly absorbed by the fair cavalieresses (if I may use such an expression) who formed the principal charm of the picture. Where all were so eminently graceful, it would seem invidious to particularise, yet I could not help gazing with peculiar delight on the majestic Countess of Northangerland, the charming princess Maria (who, by the bye, I remarked, did not look in a very good humour, for her brother, the Duke of Fidena, had insisted that only himself should ride by her rein & he kept sharp watch over her the whole time), my Cousin Julia, Ellen Grenville, the marchioness of Wellesley & many, many others. I came into the yard with Mary. Eugene Rosier, my brother's favourite page, stood by her palfrey, a magnificent creature with housings of white velvet. The lad was about to assist his lady to mount when Zamorna came up &, lifting her himself into the saddle, asked if she would like her guards to attend her in the journey.

She smiled & replied, "As you please, my lord Duke. I have no will but yours."

Turning from her a moment, he exclaimed, "Eugene, open my kennel. Let loose Roland, Roswal, Angria, Calabar, Condor & Sirius." [92]

A door in the stately stables was immediately unlocked & out sprung six noble dogs: two blood-hounds, two deer hounds & two immense newfoundlanders. Yelling & howling with joy they bounded forward, grovelled at the Duke's feet & looked up as if to receive his commands. "Guard your mistress," he said. With prompt obedience they rushed simultaneously round her &, by a variety of sounds & rapid impetuous motions, seemed to express their determination to be faithful to their precious & lovely trust. "Now unloose the other kennel," continued Zamorna.

This also was done, & with the violence of liberated tigers, a brace of mighty dogs, like Antediluvian Giants of the Canine species, rushed from their place of confinement. Both were coal black, strongly made, with truly malignant & lowering countenances, dangerous looking almost as vicious bulls. They were of that breed of dogs used at the Cape[93] for lion hunting. Each wore a steel collar round his neck, fastened with a broad & massive clasp of gold. At first they seemed rather confounded by the unexpected splendour that met their sight &, pausing in the midst of the yard, gazed round with a horridly ferocious stare, while at the same time, a leering growl rattled in their throat & breast. Some of the ladies, appalled at their formidable appearance, began to show symptoms of uneasiness at the proximity of such savage animals, & even a few of the gentlemen, such as Captain Tree & co., seemed not quite free from discomfort.

One of the mounted cavaliers, a tall man of genteel bearing & exterior, but with a countenance by no means prepossessing, a circumstance which he owed rather to the singular obliquity of his eyes than to any malformation of feature, rode up to Zamorna. "My lord Duke," said he, "those dogs appear dangerous. Would it not be better to leave them behind?"

Arthur looked at him with a haughty sneer and, with a high bred though not well bred air of contempt, turned without reply to his lovely Duchess, on the neck of whose palfrey he was leaning.

"Viscount Lofty, Viscount Lofty," exclaimed the soft, though rapid, accents of M[r] Warner, "are you afraid? If so, you had better remain at the hall yourself."

"No, M[r] Warner, I am not afraid."

"Prove it to me, my lord, prove it to me! Dare you touch the dogs?"

"Permit me to ask you the same question, sir?"

Warner dismounted from his horse, advanced towards the huge animals &, unmindful of the savage growl with which they greeted his approach, coolly & deliberately stroked their bristled backs &

heads.

"Now do the same," he said, turning triumphantly to lord Lofty.

That nobleman, thus challenged, could not refuse; he came forward with apparently as little reluctance as Warner had displayed. His hand, however, trembled as he stretched it towards the dogs. They felt the difference between his indecisive touch & the firm one that had before been laid on them, &, with a frightful yell, they sprung at once upon their prey. A cry of terror mingled with genuine Verdopolitan peals of laughter arose from the bystanders, & above all was heard the scornful & exulting ha! ha! of Zamorna echoing through the hall turrets like the laugh of a fiend. In a few seconds, however, urged by the entreaties of Mary, he sprang to the rescue.

"Down, Moloch! Down Apollyon!"[94] he shouted in a voice of thunder. "Don't stain your noble fangs in the blood of a coward!"

With the assistance of Mᵣ William Lascelles & lord Castlereagh, he succeeded in throttling them off.

"Eugene," said he, "fetch me their muzzles instantly. They have tasted blood & nothing but main force can restrain them now."

The page obeyed like lightning, &, while a few grooms conveyed off the lifeless body of lord L[ofty], who had fainted with terror but was not fatally injured, the Duke of Zamorna, kneeling on one knee in the middle of the yard, with his own royal hands fastened on the muzzles of his terrible canine favourites, Castlereagh & Lascelles (who seemed highly delighted with the whole affair &, from their reckless character & intimate knowledge of dogs, were not afraid to meddle with the fiercest) holding one while he secured the other.

"Thank you, Frederic. Thank you, William," said he, rising & casting loose the leash by which he had partly retained them from his wrist. "That will do. Moloch & Apollyon shall batten on no more cowards for a while. Why, my lords, such food as that Macara would soon melt their stout hearts to mere jelly. If, on the contrary, if I could feed them on Warners, the brisk, gallant little cock, they would be fitting blades[95] indeed." So saying, he vaulted into his saddle &, dashing his spurs to the rowels, galloped with meteor rapidity through the yard gate & down the road, which soon shook to the hoofs of two hundred steeds.

About fifteen miles from the family seat of the Percys & five from that of the Pelhams, there is a broad and beautiful valley, well wooded, fertilized by the waters of the Rio Grande[96] & embosomed in low green pastoral hills. Though the Great Road to Wellington's Glass Town[97] runs through it, it is very solitary. Some days you may sit for hours on the hills looking towards the high road without seeing anything mutable, save perhaps the shadow of a passing cloud darken its smooth & sweeping extent. In this place an incident occurred during the journey which the course of my narrative will require me to record.

Mr Warner at one period had ridden on considerably before the general party. Suddenly he was seen to stop & look earnestly in the direction of a copse by the road-side. At that moment a shrill & remarkable sound, almost like the cry uttered by a bird of prey, rang through the valley. There was something appalling in it, something that chilled the blood of every listener, & a simultaneous tightening of reins plainly revealed how universal was the feeling which it inspired. The halt, however, was but momentary.

Northangerland was the first to push forward. "What ails you all?" said he laughing aloud. "Are you startled at the whistle of a hawk?" & he pointed to one of those birds soaring high in the sunlight, but it seemed at far too great an elevation to have been the utterer of that piercing & unearthly cry. "Warner," shouted the Earl, "what is the matter with you? Are you moonstruck?" There was no answer; Warner remained still as a statue.

All now galloped up to him & at once he was assailed with a thousand questions, but he did not seem to hear one. His eyes were fixed like those of a corpse, his face pale — large drops of sweat were starting from his forehead yet there was no expression of horror in his still, mild countenance, but rather one of strange & composed solemnity.

"What can be the matter with him?" was the general question. No one could furnish an answer to it. Mysterious looks & nods were, however, exchanged between several members of the

Warner family who were present & at last Mr Charles Warner muttered, "He sees something more than we do. The second-sight is on him." ⁹⁸

These words soon passed round & there was no heart but beat faster on hearing them. Yet this was a singular scene for the second sight: in a fertile lowland country, scarcely two hours past noon, the sun yet high in heaven, no wild hills, no gloomy mists, no winds sighing through mountain gorges in cadences that might frenzy the soundest brain. Yet the novelty of the scene perhaps heightened its impressiveness. At any rate, every one's feelings were wound to the highest pitch when Warner at length broke silence.

"Gentlemen," said he, in a calm, collected tone, passing his hand over his really noble forehead, "this is a fatal gift. Where is the Duke of Zamorna?"

"Where is he?" echoed a hundred voices.

It was soon ascertained that Arthur was not amongst them, & his wife, trembling with apprehension, said that he had communicated to her his intention of not going further than the first ten miles, but that she had not seen him quit the cavalcade."

"Mr Warner," she continued earnestly & agitatedly, "if you imagine any harm has happened to him, tell me at once & do not let me remain in a state of suspense."

"My lady," he replied, "you may believe me when I say that as far as I know, none has happened. My emotion, if I displayed any, arose from awe not from horror. I merely wished to communicate to the Duke what I have just now beheld or immagined that I beheld."

"Shall not I make as good a confident as my son in law?" asked the Earl of N[orthangerland], with the most withering sneer conceivable.

"No," was the brief reply.

"& why not? You may as well tell the mumery to me as another."

Warner rose in his stirrups, fixed on Northangerland an eye that flashed like forked lightning, & exclaimed, "Northangerland, Infidel, Unbelieving Demon, farewell! You have insulted me in a way that I shall never forget!" He spurred his horse to a thundering gallop, & ere five minutes were elapsed had vanished from sight in a direction exactly opposite to Tamworth Hall.

CHAPTER THE IVth

I see the lake, the mountain rill,
Before me darkly flowing;
In the passes of the low green hill
I hear the night wind blowing.⁹⁹

Evening had fallen before our hero was so far recovered from the state of agitation into which the incidents detailed in our last chapter had thrown his irritable nerves to pay the least attention to external objects. When, however, he became sufficiently composed to look around, he perceived that the face of nature was totally altered from the scenes he had left. The path for which, in his hurry, he had forsaken the Great main road was narrow, rugged & evidently unfrequented. Grass grew on each side & in some places it stretched quite across like a level green. The low hills by which he was entirely surrounded & which shut in the view from every side bore no marks of cultivation. They were, however, very verdant, & here & there a distant flock of half-wild sheep might be described feeding in their hollows. The solitariness of the spot was heightened by the approach of twilight, by the lowering aspect of the heavens which were now covered with clouds, & by the thick & drizzly fog that was rolling down the lonely hill-sides. This prospect was no very cheering one to meet Warner's eye. He determined, however, not to return.

"I will not go back to Percy Hall," said he. "Northangerland's insult rankles in my breast like a barbed arrow. Vile sceptic, that he should dare to doubt what I have now three times proved, even in my short span of life! The supernatural gift is a heirloom which has descended to our family through many generations. Yet I could wish that the vision had not fallen upon me in such a time & place! It has exposed me to the risk of being counted an imposter, but it shall do so no more. I will never again breathe word of what I saw to mortal ear, not even to Zamorna, who would be more moved at it than most men."

The moon now at intervals began to make a faint & transient appearance in the fields of blue sky that opened to the East. Its pale & large disk shone with melancholy dimness through the cloudy atmosphere, scarcely assisting with its beams the doubtful glimmer of the fast receding twilight. Warner rode on in such a mood as the hour, the cold rain, the sad moan of the wind & the dreary darkness of the heavens were calculated to inspire. He felt deeply pensive but not unhappy, & scarcely wished to exchange the lonely solitude of his present situation for all the gaiety of the brilliant society of which a few hours before he had formed a principal member. As dusk declined to night, however, he could not help feeling some solicitude respecting a place of shelter for himself & his wearied steed.

While these cares occupied his mind, the sound of horses' feet struck his ear; the noise was evidently before him, & erelong a turn in the road brought in sight two riders. A nearer approach served to give him some idea of the identity of these belated travellers. The hind most, who from his slender form appeared as yet to be scarcely above the age of boy hood, had the appearance of being groom or page to the principal personage. He was dressed in splendid green livery & a green plume floated from his velvet bonnet. The other, a stately & majestic rider, was mounted on a magnificent black charger; two dogs of the same night like hue gallopped by his side & occasionally uttered a deep toned & subdued bay, which rung far through the night & fell with heart-smiting solemnity on the ear which the sad wind had already attuned for the reception of mournful sounds. It happened that the page had occasion to pause for a few minutes in order to adjust some part of his horse's harness that had got wrong.

Immediately the voice of his superior was heard peremptorily exclaiming, "Come on, Eugene, what are you loitering behind for?"

That voice, with its clear profound tones & imperious accent, fell famillarly on Warner's ears. "It must be the Duke of

Zamorna," he said.

Just then, his conjectures on the subject were put past all doubt by the cavalier's turning his head. There was no mistaking those features, the eye which brightened, or the curls which shadowed them. "My Lord Duke!" exclaimed Warner, spurring his steed to a gallop.

"Mr Warner!" replied Arthur, restraining his till it backened & reared with the suddenness of the check given to its spirited motions. "You here! What in the name of night & storm & darkness[100] brought you from Tamworth to this desert place?"

An explanation was soon gone into betwixt them, which concluded by the Duke's offering Mr Warner his assistance to procure him a place of shelter for the night. This offer our hero, of course, gladly accepted & both then rode on. Conversation such as two men of abilities like those we have here brought into contact would find the means of commencing & maintaining beguiled the way for some time. At length Zamorna suddenly became taciturn. He rode apart from his fellow-traveller & seemed deeply engaged in thought. They were now proceeding along the brow of a hill; their path was shadowed by lofty trees growing sometimes in thick clusters & sometimes in a more isolated & scattered manner. These occasional intervals of foliage gave to view the distant prospect, & at one wider than the rest Warner was tempted to stop in order to recconnoitre the scenery by which he was surrounded. The low aclivity that formed his station sloped into a small hollow, a sequestered & solitary spot which formerly had been entirely shut from sight by the intervening boughs of a tall chesnut. It was now hewn down & its trunk, branches & withering leaves lay prostrate: a stately ruin on the hill they had once shadowed. The gleam of a little lake was visible at the bottom of the hollow, its tiny billows glittering in the moonlight & its banks overhung by a single tree whose boughs, strangely contorted by the wind, seemed as they waved & writhed above the water almost instinct with life. At its foot lay a broken seat green with moss & weather stains. Beyond this glen & the hillocks that bounded it, a wide plain stretched, of that pastoral character which is so frequent in Wellington's land. There was a proud castellated mansion, seemingly the seat of some dominant aristocrat, embosomed in its hereditary woods, parks & lawns. Fields, orchards, cottages & a small village, distinguishable in the extreme background by its many twinkling lights, filled up the picture. All was softened & obscured by the shower of silvery dimness which the union of mist & moonlight diffused over all visible objects. Warner heeded not the rain or the cold night air as he stood gazing down on this simple scene, listening to the dreary dash of waves rushing wind-driven on the little shingly beach, the varied tones of the blast now rising in a shrill whistle & now decaying to a soft moan, watching the ghost-like shadows of clouds, as they flung a momentary & hurried gloom across the landscape & then vanished over the wild horizon, & suffering himself to be wholly absorbed in the thoughts which such a prospect naturally awakened in a mind like his.

"This is the hour, this is the scene," he muttered to himself, "in which that disembodied spirit should have appeared to me. I could meet it now & welcome it."

"What spirit?" asked the voice of Zamorna, who, unnoticed by Warner, had dismounted from his horse & stood near with folded arms & a countenance of the darkest melancholy.

"The spirt of one, my lord Duke, whom you once loved. So far I will tell you, but death should not extort another word from me. Once already to day my assertion has been doubted. I will not expose myself to such an insult a second time."

The Duke directed to Warner an eye that kindled like a star. He drew a pistol from his breast. "Sir," said he, "I will shoot you dead on the spot if you do not speak out. That pool will receive & retain your body. The land as far as you can see belongs to me & the whole country is my father's. Neither Discovery nor punishment can follow & I am determined: tell me then at once whether it was the apparition of — of — tell me, I say sir, at once, what it was you saw."

"I will not tell you," said Warner, & he too coolly produced a pistol. "My word when once passed is irrevocable. This weapon shall defend my life. Therefore, beware, my lord Duke; my eye is clear & my hand steady. Yours at this moment trembles with fury."

What Warner said was undeniable & the Duke could not but feel its force. He stood for a moment perfectly transported with passion, then, suddenly springing forward, dashed Warner's pistol from his hand, flung his own into the lake, where it fell with a sullen & heavy plunge, then remounted his horse & haughtily commanded Warner to follow him. He hesitated for some time whether he should obey, but at length reflecting on the unpleasant position in which a refusal would place him, as he was quite unacquainted with the country, & besides, being not wholly unaccustomed to these out-bursts of his youthful monarch's spirit, he determined to proceed.

"Your Grace's madness will have fatal effects sometime," said he, as he came up with him. "Why do you not strive to restrain it?"

In reply the Duke swore a deep oath & bade him be silent, as he wanted no palaver just now. But Warner was not so to be checked. He went on sternly reprimanding him for his want of self-government & remonstrating with him in terms which few others would have dared to use in his situation. Instead of being further enraged by his expostulations, Zamorna gradually regained composure; the scowl which had blackened his brow disappeared; his distended nostrils resumed their natural Appearance; & his respiration grew less rapid & irregular. This change seemed complete as they reached a large iron Gateway whose delicate & elaborate workmanship showed it to be the entrance to some Gentleman's grounds, though the mansion which they encircled was as yet concealed by the venerable groves planted round it.

"Here we find shelter," said the Duke turning to Warner with a smile, as they rode through the portal which Eugene had dismounted to open. Proceeding up a long avenue they soon reached a vacant space formed by a gravel path & two rows of flower borders planted before the windows of a handsome old Chateau, which with its embattled roof & gothic gables, grey & Ivy-grown but in a perfect state of repair, looked like the family seat of some wealthy squire, but was neither sufficiently extensive, nor sufficiently magnificent for the palace of a nobleman. With an alacrity that almost amounted to eagerness, the Duke sprang from his charger & flung the reins to his page saying, "Take Black

Afrite[101] & Mr Warner's horse to the stables, Rosier. You can find the way to the kitchen without introduction. A redundancy of diffidence I know is not one of your qualifications."

"Your Grace is perfectly right," replied the lad, "& I believe every *gentleman* has the same feelings with myself on that head."

Arthur now led the way to the front door. He opened it without the usual ceremonies of knocking or ringing & ushered Warner into a large hall, whose appearance presented a most dazzling contrast to the wet & dreary night without. A prodigious fire roared up the wide chimney, whose brilliant glow falling on pannelled walls & dark-slate pavement rendered almost needless the light of a handsome bronze lamp suspended by a chain in the centre. Chairs of polished oak were ranged all round, & on one side of the fire stood a settae[102] of the same with cushions of purple cloth. The Duke, still without giving notice of his arrival, strode to the hearth, followed by his leash of noble dogs who, roused & excited by the genial warmth, began to express their joy by fawning on him, licking his hands, rubbing their large shaggy heads against him &c., & at length became so troublesome in their gambols that he was forced to check them by a slight stroke of his riding-rod, exclaiming at the same in a rather elevated tone, "Down, sons of Satan! Savage & swarthy negros, avoid me!" Both instantly grovelled to his feet with a servility that seemed to say, "We have known discipline too well to disobey now."

Meantime the Duke's voice appeared to have roused some of the heretofore unseen inhabitants of the mansion. A light step was heard from an inner apartment. A door opened & gave admittance to a young lady whose dress, air & deportment announced the misstress of the house. She was tall, finely shaped, with very sweet & expressive features, a profusion of dark hair & a complexion of the richest brunette, which her dress of black satin with gold chain, cross & earings served well to set off. On seeing Zamorna, she sprang forward with an exclamation of joyful surprise. The presence of Warner however checked her; she paused & couloured highly.

"Hah, Mina," said the Duke, kindly taking her hand & tapping her on the neck with his glove. "How are you? Can you accommodate two tired travellers for a single night?"

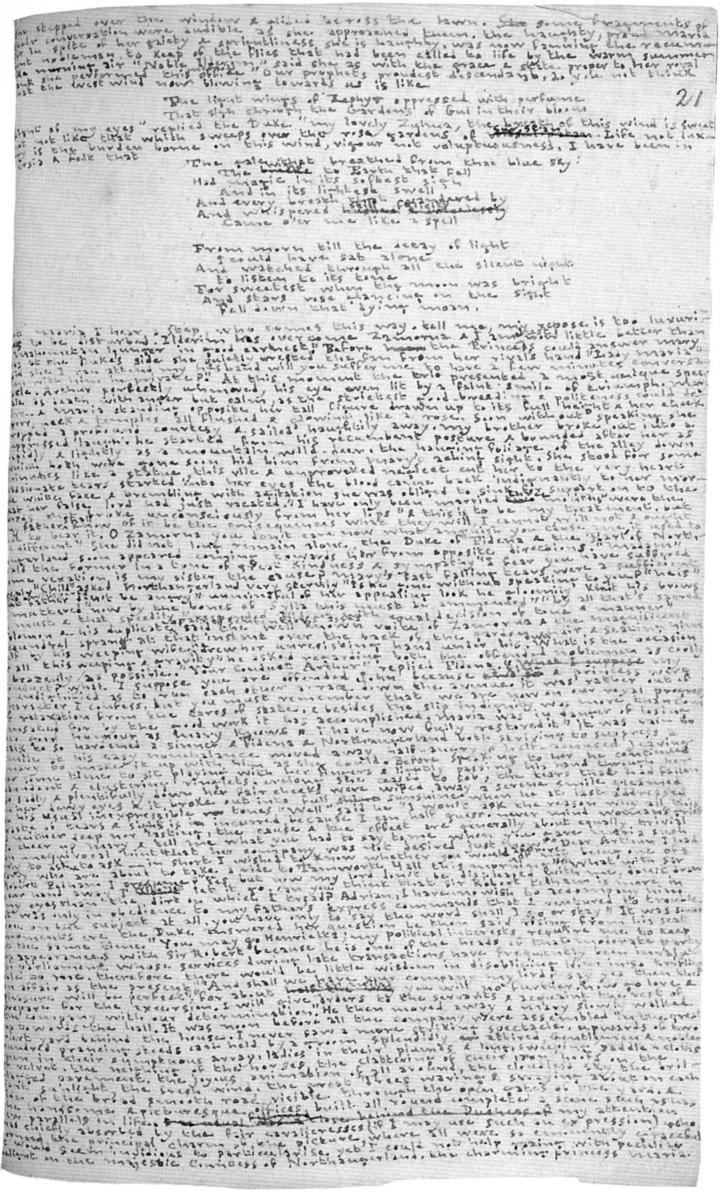

PLATE 8: Manuscript page of 'High Life In Verdopolis', illustrating Charlotte Brontë's verse interpolations that occur throughout her early prose manuscripts.

PLATE 9: 'Conway Castle', *c.*1831-1832; picturesque landscape reminiscent of the Glass Town scenery of Wellington's Land. By courtesy of the Brontë Society.

"Can I, my lord! Why, is not the house your own? I am no longer misstress when you are here, only the upper servant."

"Not so, my Girl, you are mistress both in my presence & absence. I & M' Warner will be your Guests."

"Since your Grace will have it so, permit me to perform the duties of a hostess & unclasp this dripping cloak."

Zamorna smiled & did not decline her aid as, with devoted assiduity, she disencumbered him of his heavy travelling mantle, removed his cap, whose plumes were glistening with moisture, lightly shook the rain-drops from his curls &, passing her slender fingers through the bright waves of hair, parted them from his white & lofty forehead over which they had fallen in matted clusters. A servant in the meantime rendered the same services to M' Warner. Both then followed the lady as she led the way to a large parlour, spread with fresh & brilliant carpets & furnished in a style of metropolitan elegance with mirrors, candelabra, sofas, silk hangings, &c. The Duke threw himself into an arm-chair by the fire-side & invited Warner to take the corresponding seat.

"Now, Mina," said he, "how are your young Gentlemen? Can I see them to night, or are they already retired to rest?"

"I was expecting that enquiry," replied she smiling. "They are but just gone up stairs & your Grace shall see them directly, but" (with a significant look to M' Warner) "would you wish Earnest[103] to be brought in likewise?"

"Oh! yes by all means," replied the Duke, & Mina left the apartment to obey his orders. When she was gone, Warner, whose curiosity had been considerably excited by what he had seen & heard, abruptly addressed Zamorna thus: "My lord Duke, where are we & who is that lady?"

"We are at the manor-House of Grassmere, an estate of mine in this quarter, & that lady is Miss Laury,[104] the Governante of my two — I mean of my son lord Almeda[105] & of Ernest Edward Fitzarthur,[106] a young gentleman whom I intend to bring up with Julius as his companion."

As he spoke thus the Door opened & a handsome boy about four years old, richly dressed, came running into the room accompanied by Miss Laury, who carried in her arms an infant, whose age might be near six months. She advanced with it to the Duke

&, kneeling on one knee, offered him his little bud. It looked like a scion of aristocracy, so different from the robust child of a peasant, with delicate limbs & features, a fair, transparent complexion, & tiny hands & feet as white as carved ivory. It seemed as if the plant which had borne so slight a blossom must have been itself of a tender & frail formation. Zamorna looked at it a few moments without touching it. The little thing's full dark eyes, the very counterparts of the paternal orbs that were now fixed so sadly upon it, gazed for a minute wonderingly at the stately stranger & then wandered from him to the huge dogs couched on the rug. These no sooner caught its attention than it screamed with delight & struggled to reach them. The elder boy now came up.

"Go away, mamma Mina," said he, pushing Miss Laury with all his strength.

"Give Julius to the Dogs & let me speak to this Gentleman. What do you want with us, sir? We were just going to bed when mamma sent for us down. I was sleepy & wouldn't come till she came up to fetch us herself. But I'm quite awake now, so you must talk to me & not Julius. Julius is too little to answer you."

"Humph," said Warner to himself, "I think you have as good a right to the first word as the other," & indeed the striking & undeniable similitude that existed between Ernest & the Duke justified this opinion. There was that in the child's beautiful & bold eye, patrician features, dark thick curls & already ample forehead which told of a nearer connexion than what Zamorna had intimated, & then his voice, notwithstanding its infantine lisp, had the very accent of the Duke's: the slight fall at the close of a sentence, the emphatic pronunciation, the clear though somewhat rapid utterance were all most faithfully copied, even the very melody of its tone was on the same key, though of course, several octaves higher. & when Arthur was confronted by the noble boy whose speech, look & demeanour were such perfect miniatures of his own, he acknowledged the relationship by a sudden flush which momentarily crimsoned his cheek & brow, & by the involuntary exclamation of, "Good God! How like myself!"

"Yes, I am like you," replied Ernest, "& so is little Julius, & so is the picture in mamma's broach. Who are you, Sir?"

There was no answer, the Duke only smiled.

"Who is he, mamma Mina?"

Arthur now bent down, caught him in his arms &, while he kissed him rapturously, whispered in a voice, which though low was sufficiently audible to reach the ear of Warner, "I am thy father, child."

Little Julius, who meantime had been lying on the rug, between the two gigantic hounds, pulling their long ears & grasping the rough hair of their shaggy coats with his minute fingers, in a manner that but for the noble instinct & muzzled jaws of the dogs would have provoked some retaliation, now seeing what turn matters were taking, began to display a desire of being noticed in his turn. He crept to Zamorna's feet &, nestling against them, looked earnestly up in his face.

"Little thing," said the Duke gazing down on him with a melacholy air, "do you remember me?"

A smile dimpled its small lip & cheek as if answering affirmatively to the question.

"Well then," he continued, lifting & clasping it to his breast, "I must kiss you likewise."

He silently pressed his lips to the child's forehead & then attempted to put it away, but it clung to him, hid its bright curls in his bosom & screamed passionately when Miss Laury, in obedience to the Duke's peremptory "Take him, Mina," offered to remove it. But Zamorna was now evidently becoming agitated. He thrust the infant from him, sternly bade their keeper "Take both the children away," &, rising from his seat, hurriedly paced the apartment.

Erelong he paused. "Warner," said he, "this can be of no interest to you. Excuse my neglect, but supper will be ready soon & then you will have a more agreeable employment than watching the interviews of those wholly unconnected with you. Don't think, sir, that I am ashamed of loving my children, but I am well enough aware that the expression of that love must seem foolish in the eyes of an unconcerned spectator."

"My lord Duke, I assure you it has not appeared foolish to me. I am not one of those who scorn natural affection. On the contrary, I despise & pity the man who is incapable of feeling regard for those of his own flesh & blood. How, I would ask, without the partiality incident to consanguinity, could the dignity of great & ancient families be supported?"

"Well, well," said Zamorna, "let us talk no more about it. Mr Warner, I wish to converse with you a little on the subject of my newly-obtained Kingdom. It is my desire to get all the information I can respecting its capabilities & local peculiarities. No man is so well qualified as yourself to give me that information as being the head of the oldest & most influential house in Angria. Would you favour me now with your opinion regarding the state of commerce about Mortham & the other trading towns along the banks of the Calabar?" [107]

Thus invited to pursue a theme on which his eloquence always flowed freely & willingly, Warner launched at once into his subject, which he discussed with all the energy & animation for which he is so remarkable. The Duke listened attentively, displayed great general Knowledge on the topic of conversation & asked several keen questions respecting details which, from the acute intelligence they indicated, gave Warner great pleasure in answering them.

In this manner, an hour flew by unnoticed, & our hero was almost vexed when supper was at length announced. His noble host, as they passed to the supper-room, in the most cordial & complimentary manner thanked him for the very important Knowledge he had communicated to him. Miss Laury presided at table. The Duke seemed in remarkably high spirits; he divided his attentions between her & Mr Warner, who was equally pleased with the beauty of the lady, her graceful ease & sensible conversation, & with the polished & lofty urbanity of Zamorna. Once or twice he asked himself if this could be the same person with the impetuous & passionate boy who a few hours before had threatened to murder him & throw his body into the mere. The features & form were identical, but the expression & bearing! how different!

"Truly," he thought, "I do not wonder at the magic influence which my gifted prince possesses over the female sex. He is irresistible just now, even to me, & can plainly perceive that this Miss Laury is entangled in his spells past hope of rescue."

She was indeed & her whole demeanour showed it. The manner in which she watched the direction of his eyes to anticipate his slightest wishes; her ernest attention when he spoke to Mr Warner; & her fluttering excitement when he turned his discourse to her, all too plainly whispered of a heart that had know[n] its hours of anxiety, of neglect, desertion, coldness, & was eager to enjoy in its full warmth the moment of sunshine now vouchsafed to it. My brother has nothing of the stern Bashaw[108] about him in private life. When he has ceased to care much about those with whom he has to do "he whistles them *softly* down the wind".[109] On such times as he has occasion to see & speak to them he does it as kindly as ever. Thus, like people in a consumption,[110] they flatter themselves that their case is not desperate, that his affection is reviving, & that in time perfect happiness will dawn on them again. Erelong the sickness of hope deferred comes over them. His visits become fewer & fewer, briefer & briefer, intervals of months perhaps elapse, & neither sight, sound, nor token is heard from him or of him. Meantime the poison of the deadly & venemous serpent begins to work rapidly. There is a lingering period of uttermost despair; it may be a final gleam of light when the still idolized Tyrant comes to close the dying eyes of his infatuated victims & wake a smile on the cheek of death as he whispers in those syren tones, that all along served to lure down the broad way of Destruction,[111] that he still loves them & only them. Dissolution then closes the scene & all is over. So it has been in two cases; so, I have no doubt, it will be in more. The fiend, as Northangerland said, is incurable. His qualities all show that from the first he was fated to be a splendid scourge to the world & without question he will fulfil his destiny.

After supper Miss Laury withdrew. The Duke had no sooner uttered his gentle "Good-night my Girl, sleep softly Mina & dream of me" & closed the door after her, which with condescending attention he had risen to open, than the animated light vanished from his eyes, every trace of vivacity left his features, the strain of cheerful & light conversation in which he had indulged was at once exhausted.

He turned to Mr Warner. "There," said he, "you have witnessed a piece of good acting. Mina sees me but seldom & she should have sunshine while I stay. But to speak truth, my spirits are infernally low tonight; it was like suffering the peine forte et dure[112] to rattle on in the manner I have done. Warner," he continued, "step this way a minute."

Warner obeyed. The Duke moved towards a curtain of green silk which seemed to be suspended before a recess corresponding with the bow-window in the opposite wall. He withdrew the curtain & silently pointed to a large picture that appeared behind it. It was a full length delineation of a youthful & very lovely female figure, whose delicate & refined cast of beauty derived additional interest from the touch of sadness with which it was embued. Its graceful attitude & soft rich colouring betrayed the matchless pencil of De Lisle,[113] & the bold background & exquisite finish of detail marked it as one of his master pieces.

"Do you know that picture?" asked Zamorna.

"Yes, my lord, it is the portrait of your late wife, the princess Marian. I saw her only once but her features are not easily forgotten."

"Right," he replied & abruptly dropped the veil.

"Now, Mr Warner, I ask you one thing. Was it the apparition of that lady which you saw or thought you saw?"

Warner was silent.

"Tell me," continued the Duke with increasing vehemence. "Sir, I have a dash of superstition in my mind that poetry has communicated & the idea of her spirit, which was so pure & sinless, being unable to rest burdens me more than I can express."

"My lord Duke," replied Warner, "the necessity under which I am laid of denying your request is deeply painful to me, but I said I would not utter another sentence on the subject & I never yet broke my word."

"Then you refuse me?" continued Zamorna.

"I do, my lord."

"It is well, Sir, yet observe that you are the first human being, either man or woman, who ever refused Arthur Wellesley anything after he had taken the trouble to make himself agreeable to them."

"My lord, I am proud of the distinction, but it has cost me a struggle with my feelings to gain it."

The Duke turned from him without reply. He impatiently

rung the bell. A servant presently answered the summons. "Bring my chamber lamp," said he, "& tell Rosier to follow me up stairs."

The man soon returned bearing a lighted wax-candle in a silver sconce. Zamorna, as he took it from his hand, angrily said, "Attend Mr Warner to his chamber when he requires your assistance."

He then left the room, & the sound of his haughty stride & jingling spurs soon dyed along the intricate passages of the mansion.

"When would you wish for my services, sir?" asked the footman, who was a respectable looking man about fifty years old, not at all like the fluttering & gaudy butterflies that haunt our Verdopolitan Palaces.

"I am ready now," replied Warner, "You will show me the way, I suppose?"

"Yes sir. Follow me if you please."

The chamber into which he was ushered, after ascending a broad old-fashioned staircase of waxed oak, had that air of venerable but gloomy antiquity which characterized the rest of the manor-house. The bed-hangings &c. of mulberry damask looked new & handsome, but the heavy beams of the ceiling, the wide fire-place fantastically carved, the huge mirror in a japanned frame suspended over the dressing table & a pair of large arm-chairs whose rich damask coverings could not conseal the obsolete fashion of their frames, seemed to belong to a past generation & diffused the stateliness of old times over the appartment which they adorned. As Warner's valet de chambre for the time being rendered him the duities of his station, he did not appear to think it wholly necessary, notwithstanding the gravity of his demeanour, to abstain from a little of that gossip which waiting-maids & men have from time immemorial been priveliged to indulge in.

"Well Sir," said he, "I have lived in this house for five years & I never before saw two visitors in it at once. Before Miss Laury & lord Almeda & master Fitz-Arthur came, it used to be so still from night till morning that you might hear a mouse stirring, & well it might, to be sure, for there was nobody in it but Mr Lancaster the steward, a few womenkind, the Gardener, the butler & myself."

"Do you know who that young Fitz-Arthur is?" asked Warner.
The man shook his head mysteriously.
"Is he any way related to Miss Laury?"
"Nay, Sir, that's what I can't tell. It's easier to say whether he's related to the Duke or not, for it's like, in a manner, written on his forehead. But for Miss Laury, I don't know, not I. Folks will talk, you know, & master Ernest always calls her his mamma, but then for all that she's a good lady & a kind misstress. Few that have risen as she has done have so little pride about them."
"Does the Duke often come here?"
"No, this is his first visit for nearly two years. Before he married lady Marian Hume, he used to come oftner, because the manor-house is convenient to Badey Hall,[114] & for a long while he could hardly bear [to be] out of her sight. At first she wouldn't have him, but I'll warrant you our young lord soon brought her to — poor thing, she loved him past her life all the time, but for some reason she daren't wed him.[115] They always met by the mere. Many a time on a summer's evening, about night-fall, when I was coming home from Keswick,[116] that's a little village two miles beyond Badey Hall, I've heard his whistle ring up from the glen as clear & shrill as a mavis call,[117] & then a bit after I've seen lady Marian through the trees come tripping down the hill-side like a fairy. I often wished to see their meeting, but I never dare come so near the edge of the hollow, for if Lord Douro had caught a look of me, my hash would have been settled[118] for one-while. But it's all over now. Since then she's been married, dead, buried, & he's got another wife. A beautiful woman they say & a good, heigho! I wish the Duke were steadier."
"Are you an old servant of his Grace?"
"Yes sir, that I am. I've known & served him ever since he was the size of his own bonny little sprout — I mean of my young master lord Julius — & I don't think there's another man like him in the word for twining round a body's heart, he['s] so noble & handsome & has such a winning way with him. Then he's as open-handed as the day to his own people: the tenantry of Grass-mere had forty per cent given out of their rents last half-year because they happened to be paid up on the day his son was born. But then, Sir, he's as wild as the wind, & as secret about what he

does as night. The Duchess, his mother, never as long as she lived knew him rightly. She now & then guessed that all was not as it should be, & there was one thing, I could never quite tell what, but I think it related to Miss Laury, that fretted her sadly. But his maddest tricks never reached her ear & it was well they didn't, for she couldn't have stood some of them."

"Was the Duke of Wellington acquainted with his character?"

"Aye, *he* knew him well enough, & I've heard Mr Lancaster say that once when lord Douro got desperately deep in with a set of blackguard Gamblers in Verdopolis, he swore he would disinherit him. But fortunately, the marquis soon learnt the whole mystery of that trade — for he's as keen as a knife edge & as sharp sighted as a hawk. So his father heard no more of his losses &, for the rest, he knew there wouldn't be wisdom in driving him further."

The garrulous valet, now having finished all that was required of him, took up his candle &, having bid his temporary master good-night with a low bow, left the room. Mr Warner, wearied with his long ride & with the exciting events of the day, gladly resigned himself to the comforts of cambric sheets & pillows of down. Too tired to watch the trembling shadows thrown round him by the flickering fire-light or to listen to the sound of groaning trees & melancholy wind that rushed incessantly past his chamber-window, he soon sunk into the oblivion of a slumber too profound to admit even the vagaries of a single dream, whether the unsubstantial shadow came either through the deluding portals of ivory or the prophetic gates of horn.[119]

CHAPTER THE Vth

— Pale Ghosts & bloodless shapes
Revisiting the Glimpses of the moon[120]

Sunrise, with all its flush of light & beauty, was breaking over earth & sky when Warner awoke next morning, renovated by the deep & refreshing slumbers which had fallen to his lot during the night. Voices were audible out-side his chamber-window, speaking in cheerful tones such as harmonized well with the warm sunlight & clear blue sky visible through the diamond & latticed panes. He sprang from his bed & stepping towards the casement flung it open; a subtle stream of cool air scented with dew & flowers instantly filled & purified the room. The Grass plat,[121] the shrubs, the tall trees & the flower borders on which his eye rested as he looked out wore that bright air of reviving freshness which nature usually assumes after a storm. Rain-drops filled the leaves of the plants & the foliage of the trees with millions of beaded drops of moisture, which reflected the beams of the sun & brightened their verdant hue to almost emerald brilliancy.

Figures, too, animated the landscape. Young Fitz Arthur was bounding among the Garden-paths & rolling on the wet grass-plat in company with Zamorna's mighty dogs, between whom & himself their seemed to exist a cordial & fearless intimacy. He was exercising his lungs seemingly without any particular aim in the way of uttering articulate or comprehensible words, but rather with the plain intention of hearing his own voice, so at least Warner gathered from the screams, shouts & shrill whistles uttered with a bold, decided air — quite extraordinary in one so young — with which his ears were saluted. His notes were occasionally mingled with the still shriller accents of little Julius, who appeared not far off in the arms of a young girl, seemingly his nurse. The child's kindling dark eyes were turned incessantly on his brother, whose gambols he seemed anxious to join, springing forward every moment in his nurse's arms, laughing when Ernest was knocked down by the impetuous motions of his canine playmates, & every moment pulling off the sable velvet cap crested with black plumes which covered his little curly head & flinging it towards him as if to attract his notice.

Warner could have gazed long at this cheering prospect had not his attention been diverted by a rap at the door. It was the servant who had assisted him to undress the preceding night & was now come to offer his services for the morning toilette. An hour sufficed for dressing, washing, shaving & for the arrangement of our hero's light & glossy hair, which I have observed is usually disposed with much care over his smooth open brow. These things done he descended to the breakfast-room. It was occupied by Miss Laury & the Duke, the former preparing breakfast, the latter reading. Mina extended her hand to Warner with a cordial greeting as he entered. Zamorna, scarce lifting his eyes from the book, saluted him with a cold but courteous nod. He did not speak & there dwelt on his lips that placid, unclosing expression, like the chiselled mouth of a marble statue, which he often wears when offended though not enraged, as I daresay the present Duchess & her predecessor have known & do know. He had evidently not forgotten the mortification which he had suffered last night, & his haughty unbending spirit looked full & dark through his refulgent eyes & the fringe of nearly black lashes that softened their fire as they rested composedly yet keenly on the page. When the cups &c. were arranged, Mina said in a subdued voice without addressing any one in particular, but evidently intending that he should hear, "All is now ready, shall we commence breakfast?"

The Duke took no notice of this indirect summons to the table. He sat still, one elbow on the back of the sofa & his head supported by his hand. Miss Laury seemed fully to understand his mood & his ways. She got up, placed a little stand beside him, brought his coffee, put sugar &c. into it with her own hands, & then quietly returned to her seat.

Mr Warner, who had no inclination to remain silent because of Zamorna's caprice, was beginning to converse with her when voices & the pattering of feet were heard on the gravel path without. The handsome, daring face of young Fitz-Arthur looked in through the open window amongst laurels & rose trees, & he exclaimed in his fine-toned treble, "Mamma, mamma Mina! Julius & I want to have breakfast with you this morning. Where is the gentleman?"

"Do you not see him, Ernest?" replied Miss Laury, pointing to Warner.

"No, I don't mean that person with moving blue eyes, but the tall young man in black, with long, white, fingers & brown curls, who said he was your husband."

"What did I say, Ernest?" asked Zamorna, coming forward & interposing himself as a screen between Mina, who had likewise advanced to the window, & M' Warner.

"Ah, you are there!" said the child, at once springing through the casement & seizing his hand. "You said you were mamma's husband."

The Duke silently elevated his eye-brows & threw a glance over his shoulder to Mina. How she received it I do not know, as he entirely protected her from observation.

"You little imp!" said he. "Are you establishing your claim to just & lawful succession already? What do you mean?"

"I mean that you said you were my father &, if so, you must be mamma's husband."

"Well argued," replied the Duke, sitting down & lifting the young logician on to his knee. "Eh bien, Ernest, call me mamma's husband if you will. It went very near being so at one time,¹²² but three or four other's got a finger into the pie & too many cooks, you know, Edward, spoil the dish."

"How did you know my name was Edward as well as Ernest?"

"I first chose your name, child."

"Did you? Well, & what is *your* name."

"Arthur."

"& what besides?"

"Augustus."

"& what besides that?"

"Adrian Wellesley."

"& why is not my name the same as yours & why is not mamma's name the same as yours? & why *is* Julius's name the same as yours when ours are not?"

These questions, puzzling as they were, did not seem to disconcert Zamorna. He regarded the child with a piercing look & answered somewhat sternly. "Because I ordered it otherwise. Ernest, you will remember that my orders are always to be obeyed without complaining, without questioning."

"& are you the master of this house?"

"Yes."

"I thought so, for Bessie told me that you came into it last night without knocking at the door & you look so tall & your Dogs are so large & your forehead & your eyes are so like pictures, & Black Afrite is so beautiful & now you smile like, like, in short like the only man in the world whom I will ever obey."

"& who is that, child?"

"Yourself, Sir. But where is mamma? She's gone. I thought I heard her sob as she went out. Is she angry, do you think, sir, at being called your wife?"

"Hardly, Ernest."

"Well, I should think her very hard to please if she was, for I'd rather be married to you than any body else. But look! Look at Julius! I left him on the lawn & see where he is now."

The small round face of Julius with its curls & smiling eyes actually appeared over the window sill. Impatient of remaining unnoticed without, he had climbed up the low casement which was about a foot from the ground by means of creepers & bushes & now lay on the edge in a very precarious situation. Zamorna snatched him up with an eagerness that showed how precious the little thing was to him. He kissed his delicate cheek, which the morning air had suffused with a cherub flush of crimson, & gazed fondly, yet apprehensively, on the snowy arms, neck & forehead to which his black mourning dress gave additional transparency of tint.

"I fear," he said, "thou hast too much of thy mother about thee, Julius. If I had not heard that my own frame was far from robust in infancy I should more than doubt the possibility of such a tender shoot ever becoming a tree."

A long interval of silence now ensued. The Duke had fallen into one of his moody reveries. Ernest, who stood at his knee, was employed in watching him intently. Julius, after one or two restless attempts to get first his father, & then his brother, to play with him, relapsed likewise into silence &, nestling in Zamorna's arms, erelong gave notice by his gentle breathing that he had fallen asleep. Warner did not care to break the hush of the appartment which no sound disturbed, save the song of birds & the murmur of trees in the Garden, so he took a volume of Alexander Soult's poems from the table &, sitting down near the fire, was soon absorbed in its perusal. An hour elapsed before the occurrence of any interruption. At the end of that time, a servant entered carrying a letter on a silver salver. As he presented it to the Duke, he said, "A man brought it just now from the post-office at Keswick, please your Grace. He says it was left there by one who desired it might be forwarded to Grassmere Manor House without delay."

"Very well," replied Zamorna, taking it & carelessly breaking the seal. He had not read two minutes before some strong internal emotion produced by the contents made the blood rush rapidly & darkly to his face & temples. Gently depositing the sleeping Julius on a sofa, he got up & strode through the room, a customary movement with him when violently agitated. Pausing before a window, he re-read it as if doubting the evidence of his eyes.

"Great God!" he exclaimed. "There are things on earth indeed not dreamt of in our philosophy![123] Warner, Warner" (lowering his voice) "I know your secret! But hush! Not a word! I will tell you more here after. It is as well not to speak of it at present. Your penetration will easily tell you why; there are supplanters. In the meantime, I must depart instantly. You will return with me to Percy Hall?"

"No, my lord, I cannot, the impious scepticism of Northangerland — "

"Silence! Nonsense, you *must* Go back. Northangerland will have coals of fire heaped on his head now for his unbelief! Heaven & Hell! Who would have imagined it? But Warner, I say, you don't as yet know all. You saw only the shadow of a vanished vision. Come, I shall ring the bell & order your horse."

"My lord, I will not be controlled. My determination never again to enter Percy [Hall] is fixed. I must & will abide by it!"

"What, will you give up your prize? Will you yield Ellen Grenville to Macara Lofty? By all that's sacred, he'll carry her off if she is not well watched! She's more than half his already; notwithstanding the scoundrel's base-born vile poltroonery, he has attractions of his own. Already he has contrived to poison the General's ear against you, to divide Ellen's love, to win the favour of her mother, & without a long & strong pull in which I'll heartily join, for my blue-bell *ought* not to wed a coward & *must* blossom no where but in the parterres of my court, she's gone, utterly gone, now & for ever."

This kind of reasoning prevailed. Warner's silence indicated consent to immediate departure. The Duke rang the bell till the rope broke in his hand.

"Our horses like lightning!" he exclaimed to the servant who answered his alarming summons.

Eugene Rosier presently appeared with his master's travelling cap & cloak, & those of Warner. When they were accoutred, Zamorna desired him to go & inform Miss Laury that they were going. In a few minutes, she entered the room; her face was pale & her eyes showed the traces of recent tears.

"O my lord," said she, "what a short, short time you have stayed. When will you come to Grassmere again?"

"As soon as I can, Mina, but now I must go. Farewell child; your care of my children has made me your debtor. I will pay what I owe some time. Take that as an earnest, & remember me when you see it." He removed from his neck the costly gold chain which was passed three times round it & flung it towards her, together with the splendid eye-glass set with brilliants suspended at the end. It fell at her feet. She did not notice it but, covering her face with her hands, stood silent & motionless. Presently a long choking sob broke from her & proclaimed the grief & gratitude which wrung her heart.

The Duke, who was moving away, turned back. "My dear Girl," said he, gently removing her hands from her face & wiping the tears that bathed it with his own handkerchief, "don't cry. I never like to see women's tears, however shallow the spring may be from which they rise. Nay, I did not mean to reproach *you*, *your* heart is true I know, perhaps too true. But weep no more. I'll return to Grassmere & stay a week before I leave the country. There, that's right, rose-bud, light the dew with smiles. Good bye, Mina, & bless you, my girl, for as bonny a flower as ever bloomed in a peasant's home-close, you deserved transplantation. Now, Ernest, come here. Farewell, my bold boy. Obey your mother & love her — she's worthy of it."

"I do," said Ernest. "But, sir, I shan't bid you good-bye. Sir, you said you'd come again & to make you come sooner I shall only just shake hands with you now." & he put his little palm into that of Zamorna. Then turning from him, offered it to Warner. "Sir," said he, "I haven't spoken to you much this time, but I will some other day, so come back with my Father if he'll let you."

Warner smiled & returned a suitable acknowledgement for the honour Master Fitz-Arthur's invitation had conferred on him. The Duke now folded Julius in his arms, covered him with his sable cloak for a minute, bent his stately head with all its shadowy plumes over the little creature's brow, then, laying him down without word or audible kiss, left the room. Warner followed. In three minutes their horses' hoofs were heard echoing along the gravel walks & green alleys of the lawn.

"Warner," said the Duke as the iron gate-way which terminated the grounds closed after them, "you, I know, are not the man to return ingratitude for hospitality. I request it as a favour & demand it as a right that no breath of what you have seen or heard within the boundaries of that park-wall shall ever pass your lips."

"My lord," replied Warner, "do you think I could be guilty of a breach of trust? No, the faith of my family was never stained with such a blot."

"It is well," said Zamorna, & both rode on.

I must out-strip them, & carry my readers to Percy-Hall on the back of that airborne Pegasus[124] "Fancy". The party returned from Tamworth on the morning of the succeeding day. From eleven o'clock A.M. till eight o'clock P.M. I have nothing to do with them. During that time they were mostly separate, each individual pursuing his own vagaries according as inclination or amusement led, but the fall of evening gathered them in the noble saloons of the hall, where approaching twilight & glowing fires (the chandeliers were not yet lit) so diffused alternate gloom & light of the warmest tint & finest breadth imaginable. The groups were scattered: some sat on sofa's by the marble hearths; others in antique bay windows watched the early moonlight, silvering lawn & glade, gazed on the long shadows of the trees quivering like Giant Phantoms on the park-grass, & pointed out to each other the occasional images of dear that appeared few & far between, stealing darkly accross the illuminated ground, as they wended to their spearate lairs amongst the ancestral elms & oaks of a hundred summers which rose with such solemn grandeur against the star-lit sky. With one of these groups I shall incorporate myself & hear what they say.

It consisted of the earl of Northangerland, the marchioness

of Wellesley, lady Julia Sydney & General Thornton. The marchioness, languid as usual, had just been repressing an incipient yawn. It was observed by the earl.

"Now, my lady," said he, "I know you want some amusement. Gazing on moonlight landscapes is not to your taste."

"Yes it is, Percy. I assure you, neither my mind nor eyes are insensible to the beauty of that divine scene, but then, you know, even Perfection will satiate, & I really want something more lively now. Come, my lord, you are fertile in resources, find us all some general & exciting occupation."

"Yes do," said Julia, "& whatever you suggest, I'll engage to support you. I think it should be burning my Cousin Zamorna in effigy if we could only procure his angelic image. Where on earth can he have taken himself to?"

"The lord Harry[125] only knows," answered Northangerland. "I've no doubt he's gone on one of Lucifer's own errands wherever he be. But Thornton, what has entered your head? You seem to have something to communicate."

"Nay, I was only thinking that Blind-man's-buff or Hide & seek would be as good amusements as we could find out. Rare, Stirring Games, both of them, & such as I've often played at 'in life's morning march when my spirit was young'."[126]

"A good move!" exclaimed Julia. "Why, General, the thing has quite taken my fancy. Only think, to see the attempts of the old earls Ellrington, or Lofty or Richmond or Harewood, or Sir Markham Howard there, or Bud or Gifford,[127] towards escaping from so nimble a blind man as yourself, & then to look at the primming[128] & sailing about of their stately Countesses & the solemnity of my lady Edith (Maria — provided she could have Zamorna for pursuer — would run readily enough) & the scorn of Zenobia, & the stolen glances of Ellen Grenville who would sigh to be amongst us, but wouldn't dare to come. Oh, the more I think of it, the more feasible it appears! What say you, my lord?"

"Why, my lady Julia," replied Northangerland, "there would be novelty in it, certainly, & that seems to be what you are most anxious after. Therefore, take your own course, I have no objection to be a looker-on of the sport."

"Percy!" said the marchioness. "You are surely not in earnest! Why, it would kill me to be either a spectator of or a participant in any such boy's play. No, no, find something better than that or I shall sit where I am the whole evening ennuyèe to death."

The Earl sat in silent reflection for a minute. He then said, "Well my lady, I think I have found something that will please you. About ten years since there was a grand masquerade given in this house. The disguises worn on the occasion are still preserved in a wardrobe up-stairs. What say you to an impromptu masque? We could assume our dominos[129] & so-forth in a moment."

"Admirable!" exclaimed the marchioness, & "Admirable!" echoed Julia.

"Very good," observed the General.

All rose from their seats. The proposal soon spread through the rooms & was received with unanimous approbation. In ten minutes they were empty. Every soul, both young & old, had hastened to the upper-chambers & were now engaged in tricking themselves out so as best to conceal their identity. As I walked in the halls below, there was such a busy sound above my head of trampling feet & murmuring voices, steps passing hurridly through corridors, ringing of bells for waiting-maids, valets, &c. In going out for an instant on to the lawn, I could see a hundred lights gliding from window to window, now hidden by an intervening form, then again revealed with increase of brightness; sometimes disappearing altogether & reappearing after an interval in a neighbouring chamber. All betokened happy & exhilerating confusion, &, filled with joyous emotions, I returned to the house.

A flood of lustre now filled the saloons; every chandelier blazed like a sun in its own circle of silver lamps. The masquers had begun to drop in one by one. First came a lofty & most commanding figure, attired in a dress which, though of modern cut, had a singularly wild & impressive aspect: the pantaloons were white, the vest dark; a red belt girt his loins & a silk handkerchief of the same bloody hue was knotted dashingly round his head. Between the b[r]ows & from under the mask, auburn curls clustered profusely. On one arm there was a scarlet badge bearing the words "sea-man of the *Red-rover*"[130] lettered in black. Of course, I knew Northangerland, &, as he passed by, a terrible & awful vision, I thought how vast must be the power & how unbounded the audacity of that man who could thus unchecked & unfearingly make open boast of crimes that would have brought a hundred men of less intellect to the Gallows. A lady leant on his arm. By her slow yet graceful step & languishing blue eye, I knew her to be my aunt, the marchioness of Wellesley. A sea-green robe & a wreath of white & scarlet coral denoted her character to be that of a Nereid.[131] Many more followed in all the fantastic dresses that imagination can conceive; some I knew, others were too well disguised to be recognized. Amongst the former were Lord Jordan in Turkish caftan & Turban, with a rich scymitar at his side; Theresa Warner in an oriental shawl Dress with Persian drawers; Mr Montmorency wearing his counsellor's wig & gown; his daughter Julia decked out like a stately court-lady of former times; the Countess of Northangerland wrapped closely in a black cloak with a horseman's helmet & rustling plumes on her head. As she passed me, I half-imagined it was my brother, but the stature & step, though both were stately, had not quite sufficient of haughtiness & lofty bounding spring to support the delusion, at least in eyes so keen as mine. There too was Dr Stanhope, wearing a bishop's mitre & ample lawn sleeves. The Revd Henry Warner cracking a hunting-whip & singing out Tally ho! Dr Porteus in Archi-Episcopal decorations.[132] Father Pisani, the Catholic chaplain of lord Jordan, attired like an officer of the horse-guards. I beheld the hearty countenance of General Thornton under the cowl of a monk; the sweet lips & merry eyes of lady Julia looked out from a noviciate's veil; Maria Sneachie wore the coquettish mantilla of a Spanish-Donna, her black basquina[133] & graceful fan; the Royal Edith sailed by in widow's weeds; & Ellen Grenville tripped lightly on with the green tunic & gilded quiver of a huntress. It was a splendid & bewildering pageant. I seemed in a dream as I wandered slowly though the costumes of all nations, times & kindreds. Buried ages rose before me, the years of Europe's bright noon-day, of Africa's star-less night. Many of the dresses were historical & they bore me to the old cathedrals, the decayed abbeys of England, the silent churches of Spain, the viny ruins of Italy, the streams, the battle-plains & the fertile-hills of Degenerate Portugal.

But amongst the figures that surrounded me, there was one which my eye continually singled out & which, though the ideas which it suggested were by no means pleasant, I could not but abstain from watching. I had not observed it till some-time after the general re-assembling of the company in the drawing-rooms. It was then standing alone near a window rather in the shade, gazing on all who crossed its path, but speaking to none. The disguise in which it was envelloped had a strange, solemn appearance, totally out of character with all the others, & such I thought as none but a morbid or singularly eccentric mind would have chosen for a festal Party, being, in short, nothing more nor less than a cold, glazed, swathed and snow-white shroud, covering all the limbs, the head, the neck, surrounding the face with its crimped border & leaving nothing visible save a pair of glittering, bright blue eyes whose orbs were remarkably prominent & startling. This phantom, for so it looked rather than a being of Earth, stole among the merry masquers, speechless & with unechoing tread. Like cardinal Beaufort it made no sign;[134] its hands were never once protruded from beneath the shroud; its head never turned or bowed; all, in fact, except the gliding feet was as motionless as a dead & buried corpse. Many of those present noticed it beside myself & not a few addressed it, but vainly; it answered them never by words & seldom even by a glance. Amongst others there was a tall masque in the dress of an Indian necromancer who came up & stood directly before it.

"Apparition," said he, "whether thou be'est from Heaven or Hell, halt! Power is given to me among spirits to bind & loose whom I will. Whence comest thou & whither goest thou?"

Unheedingly the shroud was flitting by when the necromancer spread out his broad robes traced with occult & mystic symbols &, lifting his wand, repeated in a loud voice, "Halt! Gaze on the insignia of my power: these garments which were woven in no mortal loom; this wand which grew on no earthly tree. Silent Spirit! Phantoms of the Deep, Demons of the world that lies below the deep, bright visions of the realm that rests & shines far above, all have come when this wand rose and when these

PLATE 10: Watercolour by Charlotte Brontë, *c*.1834, after William Finden's engraving of Byron's 'Maid of Saragoza'; a source of inspiration for the Angrian heroine, Mina Laury. By courtesy of the Brontë Society.

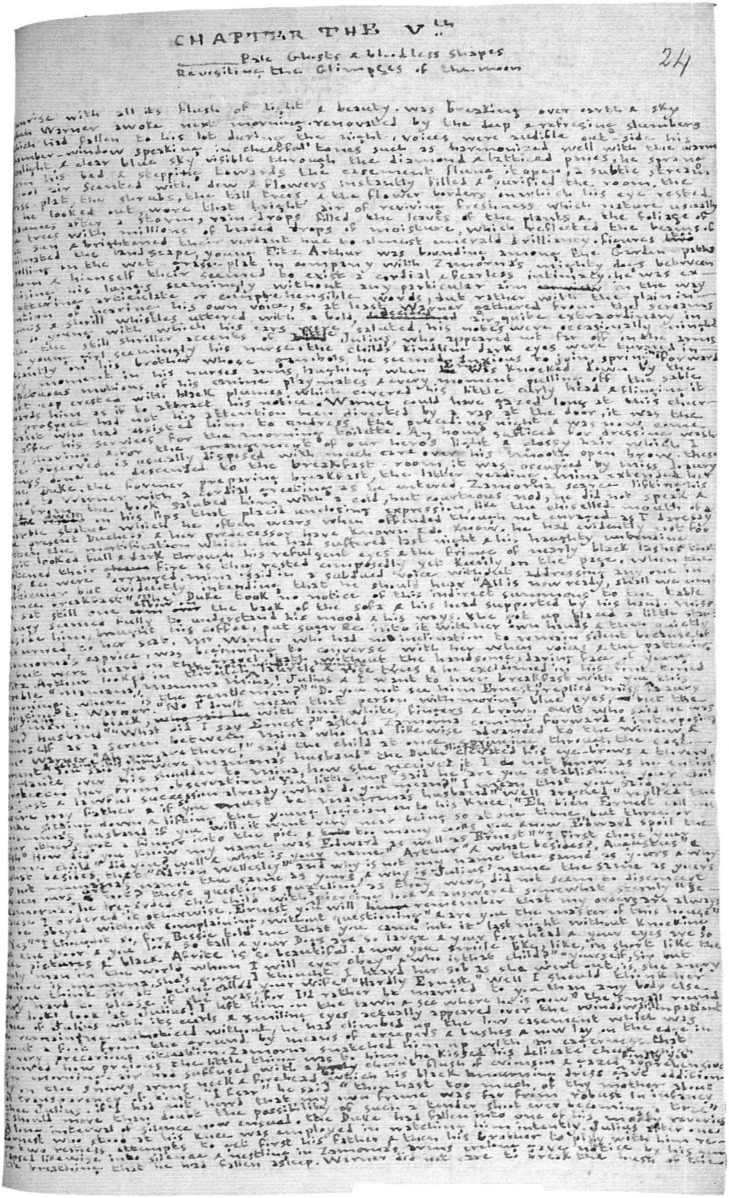
CHAPTER THE Vth

Pale Ghosts & bloodless shapes
Revisiting the Glimpses of the moon

24

PLATE 11: First page of Chapter 5 of the manuscript
'High Life In Verdopolis'.

garments waved. & dost thou — solitary, isolated, voiceless — wandering alone on earth, dost thou resist?"

A faint sound now seemed to issue from the folds of the shroud like a decaying breeze. Almost every one in the saloon heard it, for a profound silence had fallen unconsciously on all. No articulate sentence followed, however, & the whisper dyed to deeper stillness.

"Fiend!" said the magician. "Answer me, what disturbed thy rest? Was the grave too cold, the vault & earth too damp, the worms too eager? Show thy dainty limbs, spirit. Are they fair as in life? Is there no charnel scent about them, no livid traces of corruption?"

"There have been," replied a low & knell-like voice, & at the same instant the winding-sheet fluttered as if that within was convulsed by a strong & sudden shudder. The necromancer started back an instant. It seemed as if the tones had daunted him, but presently he spoke again.

"& what unsealed the sepulchre & screwed off the coffin-lid & bade the dead come forth?" he asked briefly & somewhat sullenly.

"Love," was the reply in a softer & less thrilling voice than before, & the ghost rolled its blue eyes round the circle which encompassed [it] as if in search of some one.

"Ha! Do I guess rightly?" muttered the necromancer. "But farewell, spirit, I have perhaps raised what I cannot lay."

He turned away, slunk into the crowd of bystanders &, mingling with them, disappeared. Many now gathered about the shroud, prompted by curiousity, though other feelings would have induced them to shun it. Questions were asked by some of the boldest, but its time of communion was now passed: it neither noticed nor answered them. The Seaman of the *Red-Rover* now advanced.

"Sir," said he, "you have played your part long enough. Have done with this mummery & show your face." He stretched out his arm to seize the spectre, but it eluded his grasp, darted like an arrow from him, passed without hindrance among the astonished crowd, & finally escaped through a glass door that was open to admit air to the thronged appartments.

CHAPTER THE VIth

He comes! the conquering hero comes! [135]
Mourning Bride

There was one inhabitant of Percy-Hall, the fairest of the fair, the noblest of the noble, who had not mingled in the train of revellers that filled its gay saloons. I mean the Duchess of Zamorna. Her mind, naturally sensitive, had been deeply impressed by the incident which had occurred on the previous day in the vale of Rio Grande, & though Warner had declared that he had seen nothing indicating evil to the Duke, yet she could not get rid of the idea that all was not well with him. Then, too, she feared that he might be displeased at her having accompanied Sir Robert Pelham. This notion having once entered her mind, it was impossible to drive it out; it haunted & tormented her. She longed most ardently to see him, to learn from his own lips that he was not offended, to be certain that he was well & unharmed. All day she listened for his footsteps & as twilight drew on, her anxiety deepened. At all times from her exclusive & reserved temperament averse to mingling largely in miscellaneous company, she this evening felt more than usually disinclined for gaiety, so while the rest were preparing for the extempore masquerade, she stole out to take a walk in the solitary park attended by her faithful guard, Roland. Long & pensively she strayed down the green glades, chosing such as were most sequestered & carefully avoiding the more open parts where she might be seen from the house.

The tracks she followed led her at length to the wicket gate of that church-yard so sweetly described by Flower. [136] She paused a moment before entering it; it was a solemn hour to go along among the silent dwellings of the Dead, the graves of those of her own house. But Mary's mind was at present in that state which best harmonizes with mournful thoughts. She lifted the wicket-catch & entered. The little church stood right before her, grey & hoar in the moonlight. On the green enclosure round, only three tombs appeared, but each was of marble, classic in design & grandly shadowed by the prodigious elms under which they rested.

Here slept the mortal remains of the first Percy, a great but bad man, whose death, however, was horrible enough to have atoned for many crimes. Here, too, reposed Maria di Segovia,[137] who in her life was a true daughter of the bright clime where her parents, if not herself, first received the gift of being. Lovely, ardent & impassioned, but proud, haughty, & resentful. The central tomb, white as snow, whose urn gleamed like a spirit in the trembling rays that fell on it through the boughs & foliage of its mighty canopy, covered the dust of Mary's own mother,[138] & towards it she glided with the step of a night-wandering fairy, as light, as silent, scarcely dispersing the dew which gleamed on the church-yard grass or crushing the closed bud of a single wild-flower.

She sat down on the polished slab & leaned her head against the urn; every thing was mute around her, no moan of wind however faint, however quickly passing into silence, wailed through the elm-groves or rustled the ivy that hung like a black scutcheon over the church porch. The sky above was of the deepest, stillest & most stainless blue; it looked most sublimely lofty, so that the thoughts were carried away to illimitated[139] space when gazing at it, & the radiant moon & stars from their unclouded lustre seemed floating between heaven & earth in an atmosphere of their own. Henrietta's soul, of as pure an essence as was ever enshrined in clay, could fully warmly unfold itself to all the placid beauty of the scene. Her fine eyes gazed upon it with a look of almost inspired yet tranquil rapture; calm feelings stole over her heart & soothed the anxiety which had filled it. She thought of Zamorna, still sadly, but not miserably.

All at once a step broke the holy hush of her retreat. Roland sprang up. A dark figure of the stateliest height appeared at the wicket; it was dashed impetuously open, the figure bounded deer-like forward, &, before Mary was aware, almost before she could look up, she was clasped in the arms of her own young noble worshipped lord.

"Arthur, my *own* Arthur," she exclaimed, as soon as she could find voice to speak. "Where have you been all this time? A few hours' separation is torture to me, I began to fear — ". She was going on but observed that he did not appear to listen. He had relaxed his fervent embrace and now held her from him & perused her features with a glance of the most blighting keenness. He said at last, "This is a mistake! The shadow of the tree occasioned it. Good Good!¹⁴⁰ It may be a delusion after all!" These words were sufficient to inform Mary that she was not the person whom the Duke had expected to meet in the church yard & that his cordial salutation was intended for some one else. The bitterness of this discovery entered into her soul like iron. Sick at heart, she turned away & faintly endeavoured to extricate herself from the slight hold which he yet retained on her arm. He tightened it, however, on feeling her efforts to escape.

"What, Mary?" said he. "Are you afraid of your own husband?"

"Afraid! Oh Zamorna! How can I be afraid of *you*? But I thought that I was an intruder. That you had expected some one else & would rather not have found me here."

"Well, I don't know but you may be right," he replied, drawing her towards him & smiling with a sweetness that went to Henrietta's chilled heart like a warm sunbeam. "I certainly did expect some one else, & as certainly I would rather not find my Mary in a cold church-yard on a dewy night. It seems as if the spirit was sad that wanders so from society to loneliness. Now speak truth, Henrietta. Are there not thoughts of jealousy in that little head of thine?"

"Not now, Arthur."

"But sometimes, when I am away for a few consecutive days, or when I dance twice on the same night with one lady, or when I call some tall girl with black hair & Georgian eyes my lovely Zulma, or give a certain learned Countess my arm & hail her as the Empress of Women. Yes, I see it is so, that wince tells the secret plainly. Now to probe the wound further, did you not think this very night that you had met me in a rival's stead?"

"I confess I did."

"& who may I ask was marked out as the favoured damsel?"

"Lady Maria Sneachie came for a moment across my mind."

"Ha! Ha! Ha! Well done! Poor Maria, she would be mad after me indeed, if she gave me a rendezvous by your mother's tomb-stone. But hush! By Heaven! They are here, it is true. The Dead live; the lost are found."

Just then, two figures appeared at the wicket, but so great was the obscurity of boughs where they stood that Mary could discern them only as dark outlines. The Duke flung her from him & rushed forward. She could see that one of the figures was again & again encircled in his embrace & that it returned it with equal warmth. She could hear a voice say in tones of the deepest emotion, "My dear, noble Adrian, to meet you so is worth living again for."

"Living again for," she repeated to herself. "Who can it be? Surely not, not — " A name was on her tongue, but she dared not utter it. The Duke now repeated her name & pointed towards her. She listened eagerly, but he spoke low so that nothing more was audible. Trembling with excitement, & that not of the most pleasurable kind, she determined to end her suspense by advancing nearer. Still it was in vain. Zamorna stood between her & the object of her curiousity, & his tall person & towering plumes entirely shielded the stranger from view. All three were speaking at once in rapid, earnest & subdued accents, & Mary, to her horror, amongst the confusion of voices could distinctly hear one soft feminine sound ("quiet & low, an excellent thing in woman")[141] but, silvery as it was, it smote her heart like a death-knell. In the midst of their conference, while all was silent around, save that hushed murmur of tongues, a sound broke the still, breezeless night, whose contrasting loudness produced an effect more awful than words can describe. It was the report of a pistol discharged near at hand, evidently, in fact, from behind the trees that shut in the burial-ground.

Mary saw Zamorna start back; at one bound she reached him. "My lord, are you hurt?"

"Hurt! No, love, nor are any of us, but that was no fault of the scoundrel who marked us. A curl is gone from my temples, &" (pressing her panting to his bosom) "my Mary has been frightened. For this beating of pulse & heart the assassin shall pay! Remain here, all three of you, till I call."

The Duke Dashed off in the direction whence the report had come & Henrietta was left alone with the two strangers. No pen can express the delicious relief which she experienced when on looking round she perceived that both were men: in one she instantly recognized M' Warner, whose presence accounted for the soft voice that had alarmed her so much; the other was unknown to her.

"My lady Duchess," said Warner politely, offering her the support of his arm. "Be composed, I have no doubt his Grace will sufficiently chastise the villain who has alarmed you so. I can guess by whom the act was perpetrated, cannot you, Sir?"

"Yes," replied the stranger. "My opinion on that head is so decided that I could almost take oath on the strength of it. But hist! Adrian calls."

At that moment, Zamorna's voice exclaimed from a distance, "Gentlemen, hither, the game is hunted down & a pretty fox it turns out to be."

Both obeyed the summons & Mary was again alone, but she did not long remain so. They soon returned bearing between them a man whose dark figured garments, broken wand & black mask proclaimed him to be our friend the Indian necromancer.

"Is he dead, think you?" asked the unknown, as for an instant they rested their apparantly lifeless burden on the church-yard wall.

"No," replied the Duke. "He's only shaming death to excite pity. I gave him a tolerably tight squeeze round the throat, but not sufficiently so to cheat the hang-man. Heave him up. We'll carry him into the Hall, through the saloon windows. Mary, wrap yourself in my cloak — you are shivering, child — & follow as fast as you can."

He stripped off his mantle & folded it tenderly round her. Thus disencumbered, he drew up his splendid figure to its utmost height, cast down a slight glance at the exquisitely symmetrical limb & fine, small foot by which it was terminated, stooped, lifted lightly in his arms the motionless magician, swung him round to gather force, & then flung the body like a stone from a sling to the distance of twenty yards. All this was done with an absence of effort that showed his muscular force. A groan burst from the miserable wretch as he fell. It was answered by the fierce pitiless laugh of Zamorna.

"Ha!" he shouted. "There's life yet in the vile carcase is there? Come, gentlemen, we must preserve the spark that remains to have a more ignominious quenching here after."

Again he lifted his victim &, assisted by the two others, bore him the rest of the distance to the house. They paused before the Glass door, which, as I have before mentioned, was open in one of the saloons.

"Shall we all enter together?" asked the stranger.

"Yes," said the Duke.

He pushed back the door & they stepped at once into the gay crowd & dazzling light that fluttered & glowed within. The surprise of all may be conceived at their sudden appearance, with what seemed a dead body between them. Scores flocked round, as in no gentle manner they dropped their burden on the ground.

"What have you here, Zamorna?" asked the tall seaman of the *red Rover*, removing his mask. "I said you were gone on some fiend's errand, & it seems I was right — for," he continued, fixing his eyes on the stranger, "you have brought a disembodied soul back from his place."

"Let us have no mumery, my lord Northangerland," observed Mr Warner, with marked emphasis.

"Silence, prating fool!" said the Earl. "This is a strange piece of business, Zamorna, what does it all mean?"

The Duke was silent. Many now seemed to be recognizing some former acquaintance in the unknown. The breathing of the by-standers grew thick & hurried; half smothered exclamations were heard; the ladies' cheeks & lips turned pale. A bustle became audible in the throng. A tall female figure in black came forward; the phantom advanced, caught her in his arms. There were a few sobs, a long embrace & then the words "My living Frederic", "My faithful Edith" found way, but were instantly lost in the loud thunder of applause that followed. When the general excitement had in some measure subsided, a thousand questions were at once poured out on the noble dead alive. His explanations were soon given. I shall conclude my work with a brief summary of them.

Frederic, Viscount Lofty, was, as all my readers know, numbered amongst the slain in the glorious battle of Velino,[142] & after several vain attempts to revive him, he was buried by his friend, the Duke of Zamorna, at midnight in the church-yard of a small village near the field of action. How long he lay in the grave he could not himself tell, but, on waking from his trance, he found himself lying on a heap of earth, a church spire before him, a broken coffin with the lid wrenched off beside him, & a moonlight sky above him. Erelong a harsh voice grated on his ear & the hideous figure of Robert Sdeath[143] presented itself. It is well known that this old wretch made it a practice, during the whole time of the war, to repair on the night after a battle to the places w[h]ere the dead Soldiers had been deposited &, Ghoul-like, to dig up their graves for the purpose absolutely of battening on the corpses contained within. What motive actuated him on this occasion none but himself can tell, but, instead of extinguishing the small remains of life that yet lingered in lord Lofty, he actively set about the means of prolonging & strengthening it. He carried him to the house of a surgeon & had his wound examined, when it was found that the shot which had been supposed to have perforated his heart in reality missed it by about a hair's breadth, & thus, in accordance to those laws of existence peculiar to our nation, Death had been averted.[144]

The viscount wished to send immediate information of this state of matters to his family, but Sdeath strictly prohibited it, &, as he was at present unable to act for himself, submission necessarily followed. So severe were his wounds that three months elapsed before he could rise from his bed & half a year before he could return to Verdopolis. On arriving there he found that all the members of his house had accompanied the youthful monarch of Angria to Wellington's land. Anxious to see his affianced bride, the lady Edith, his bosom friend Zamorna, his parents & his sisters (of his brother he said nothing), he determined to follow them. By rapid travelling he arrived there the day after them. He was on his way to Percy-Hall when Warner saw him in the vale of Rio Grande. Perceiving that he was looked upon in the light of an apparition, he determined to humour the idea &, plunging into a copse by the road side, disappeared before the rest of the cavalcade came up. Afterwards, having by chance taken the road which led to Keswick, the village near Grassmere, he there learnt, as news of that sort flies fast amongst country-people, that the Duke of Zamorna had arrived at the manor-house. He immedi-

PLATE 12: 'Alexander Soult', 15 October 1833; Charlotte Brontë's pencil drawing of a Glass Town poet, based on an engraving of Lord Byron in *The Literary Souvenir* for 1830. By kind permission of private owner.

PLATE 13: 'Landscape of tower and river', *c.*October 1832; inkwash on paper by Charlotte Brontë. By courtesy of the Brontë Society.

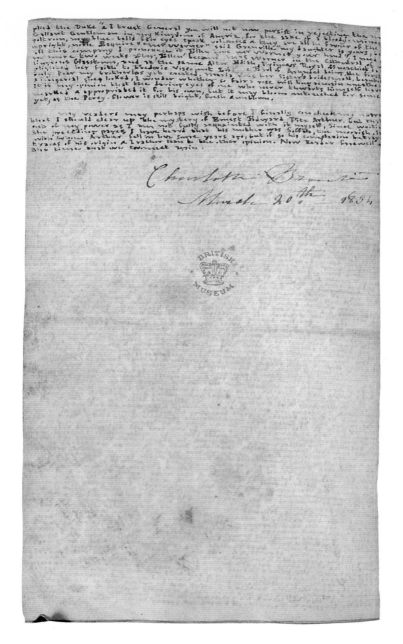

PLATE 14: Final manuscript page of 'High Life In Verdopolis'.

ately wrote a letter acquainting him with his reviiification & appointing the churchyard at Percy-Hall, which, though like many others he had never seen, Flower's Novel had well acquainted him with it as a place of meeting.

He arrived there long before his friend &, to pass away the time, amused himself by wandering before the windows of the house, hoping to catch a glimpse of the princess Edith. Happening to be at one time near that where Northangerland sat, he overheard his proposal respecting the masquerade. Being young, thoughtless, & of that disposition which delights in turning serious things into a joke, he determined to assume some disguise if possible & mingle with the other masquers. Accordingly, he stole in through the glass-door which has already been twice mentioned, followed the company up-stairs, chose out the shroud from the infinte variety of costumes with which the wardrobes were stored & (to use his own expression) "played out the rest of the game as skilfully as a dead man could manage it."

This explanation was as satisfactory as could be desired. It now only remained to reveal the person of the Necromancer, of whose dastardly conduct the guests were likewise briefly informed, but unhappily, he was nowhere to be found. While Lord Frederic was speaking, he had been totally neglected, & the wretch, taking advantage of this circumstance, had gathered up his crushed limbs & escaped. Zamorna swore like a trooper when this was ascertained. Frederic joined him every minute with a deeply muttered oath, & Warner dashed his hand against his brow & turned pale with rage.

At length the last mentioned started forward. "My lords & Gentlemen," said he, "I will tell you who the masked villain is. He bears the degraded, base, blotted & trampled name of Macara Lofty. Yes, he recognized his noble brother, &, fearful that he might claim his rights of succession & superior rank, he took that vile & cowardly method of removing him before any one else should learn his existence. General Grenville, you look astonished, but so it is. I appeal to Zamorna if I have not spoken truth."

"Heaven's truth," replied the Duke. "& I trust, General, you will not now persist in rejecting the most Gallant Gentleman in my

Kingdom of Angria, for the sake of a bloody-minded poltroon.[145]
My blue-bell's fair eyes speak volumes & they are all in favour of
the brave, upright, noble Esquire."

"Mr Warner," said Grenville, "my daughter is yours. Before
all this company, I pronounce it. Ellen, give Mr Warner your
hand."

I need say no more. Two weeks after, Ellen became M^{rs}
Warner in the Cathedral of Wellington's Glasstown. & at the
same Altar, Edith, Princess Royal of Sneachie's land, plighted
her faith to Frederic, Viscount Lofty & Earl of Arundel,[146] being
the first & only Peer my brother has yet created. Maria was her
Sister's bridesmaid; beautiful & imperial she looked. I wonder
whether so fair a rose will long remain ungathered. It is my
opinion that the daring eyes of one who never thwarts himself have
marked & appropriated it for his own, but it may bloom untouched
for some time yet, as the Percy-flower is still bright, fresh &
unblown.[147]

My readers may perhaps wish, before I finally conclude my
narrative, that I should clear up the mystery of Ernest Edward Fitz
Arthur, but that is out of my power, as I am not fully acquainted
with it myself. Since writing the preceding pages, I have heard
that his mother was Soffala, the moorish lady with whom Arthur
fell in love some years ago, but if so, his complexion betrays no
traces of his origin, & I rather lean to the other opinion.[148] Now
Reader, farewell, until the time that we two meet again

Charlotte Brontë
March 20th — 1834

NOTES

1 *Lord C A F Wellesley*: Lord Charles Albert Florian Wellesley, 'author' of this manuscript and young brother of Arthur Wellesley, Marquis of Douro, Duke of Zamorna and King of Angria. By 1834, when *High Life In Verdopolis* was written, he is Charlotte Brontë's only pseudonym and later becomes her cynical narrator Charles Townshend.

2 *'Much cry and little wool ... shearing the Hog'*: proverbial equivalent of 'all talk and no do' or 'much ado about nothing'; used again in *Villette*, vol. III, ch. 40. The original proverb went, 'Great cry and little wool, as the Devil said when he sheared the hogs.'

3 *'A Gladder day ... shone o'er fair women & brave men'*: cf. Byron, *Childe Harold's Pilgrimage*, III, xxi:

> There was a sound of revelry by night,
> And Belgium's capital had gather'd then
> Her Beauty and her Chivalry, and bright
> The lamps shone o'er fair women and brave men.

4 *Northangerland*: Alexander Percy, Lord Ellrington, Duke of Northangerland; former pirate ('Rogue'), arch demagogue, revolutionary and politician, he is first friend and then foe of Zamorna, whose third wife is Northangerland's daughter Mary. He becomes Branwell Brontë's favourite pseudonym and the central figure in his poetry and prose (*see* Introduction).

5 *the broad & downward, or the narrow & ascending path*: cf. Matthew, vii, 13-14.

6 *Fidena*: Prince John Augustus Sneachi (also Sneaky or Sneachie), Duke of Fidena, eldest son and heir of Alexander Sneachi, King of Sneachiesland. Fidena is not a member of Zamorna's Angrian coterie; yet despite this and his antipathy to Zamorna's character, Fidena is Zamorna's most respected and trusted friend.

7 *Thornton*: Thornton Wilkin (or Wilson) Sneachi, now General Thornton; brother to the Duke of Fidena, the Princesses Edith and Maria Sneachi, and second son of the King of Sneachiesland, disowned by his family because of his early 'immoral' conduct. Thornton and Fidena, whose characters are antipathetic, are not on speaking terms although both claim the friendship of Zamorna.

8 *Warner*: Warner Howard Warner, prime minister of Angria and head of the oldest and most influential Angrian family of Warners, Howards and

Agars. A contemporary and important ally of Zamorna, his relationship with his monarch is similar to that between the historical Duke of Wellington and Sir Robert Peel, on whom Warner is based.

9 *Castlereagh*: Frederick Stuart, Viscount Castlereagh, a dandified early friend of Zamorna, who becomes Earl of Stuartville and an Angrian minister after the creation of Angria. Based on Robert Stewart, Lord Castlereagh, distinguished British statesman, who was born in Ireland in the same year as the Duke of Wellington and constantly promoted his friend Arthur Wellesley's career.

10 *Lofty*: Lord Frederic Lofty, a close friend of Zamorna, who later creates him Viscount Frederic Lofty, Earl of Arundel (n. 146 below), and 'Grand Chamberlain of Angria', is an accomplished horseman (nicknamed 'The Chevalier') and popular Field-Marshal in the Angrian army. At the opening of this story, Lofty is thought to have died on the battlefield at Velino, during the War of Encroachment in which Zamorna won the kingdom of Angria. His younger brother, Macara Lofty, a Verdopolitan scoundrel, has recently inherited his title.

11 *Tree's 'Verdopolitan Magazine'*: successor to the Verdopolitan 'Blackwood's Young Men's Magazine'; 'edited' by Captain Tree, a rival novelist of Lord Charles Wellesley and early pseudonym of Charlotte Brontë. Although intended to be a 'Tory' production created in opposition to Branwell Brontë's 'The Monthly Intelligencer' (the Verdopolitan equivalent of the *Quarterly Review*), it may never have existed since no evidence of manuscripts has come to light.

12 *Zamorna's impetuous pen*: among the many attributes of Charlotte Brontë's favourite hero Arthur Wellesley, Marquis of Douro, Duke of Zamorna and King of Angria, is that of accomplished author. His preference is for writing poetry, but he occasionally publishes anonymous articles for political propaganda or to counteract the libellous accusations of his brother Lord Charles. *See* the Introduction to this volume for a discussion of Zamorna's character.

13 *Ebor Terrace*: in Verdopolis, capital of the Verdopolitan Federation, the original Glass Town (or 'Glasstown') Federation of four kingdoms with a federal capital, of which Zamorna later claims membership for his new kingdom of Angria.

14 *middle of February 1834*: the manuscript was begun on 20 February, 1834 (*see* note 18 below); Charlotte Brontë frequently set her stories at the time of composition.

15 *my friend General Thornton*: Lord Charles Wellesley has recently been placed under the guardianship of General Thornton, since Zamorna could no longer tolerate his younger brother's watchful eye and the subsequent literary reports on his behaviour. Nevertheless Lord Charles still has his apartments in Wellesley House, his father's home in Verdopolis.

16 *Daughter of the Arch*: cf. Sir Walter Scott's *Count Robert of Paris*, where Echo is referred to as 'Daughter of the Imperial arch'.

17 *headless*: stupid, brainless (OED); although transcription of this word is difficult, the reading appears to be 'headless' rather than 'heedless'.

18 *then* – : the words 'Begun February 20th 1834', written in Charlotte Brontë's cursive script, appear here at the foot of the manuscript page: *see* note 14 above.

19 *Duchess*: Mary Henrietta Percy, Duchess of Zamorna, Queen of Angria, daughter of Northangerland and third wife of Zamorna.

20 *Sanctum Sanctorum*: Latin for Holy of Holies; its usage here indicates the precociousness and pretentiousness of the youthful narrator.

21 *fauteuil*: arm-chair; a French word commonly used in English at the time.

22 *ne'er-do weel*: good-for-nothing, disreputable person. Northern and Scottish dialect, though the form 'weel' was frequently used even by southern writers such as Dickens (OED).

23 *St Augustin's Cathedral ... St Michael's*: the two cathedrals of Verdopolis, modelled on London's St Pauls Cathedral and Westminster Abbey. Like the latter, St Michael's is the place of coronation and also contains the Royal vaults. The name was probably derived from Haworth parish church of St Michael's and All Angels, of which Mr Brontë was rector.

24 *other Folks being no better worth pleasing than himself*: reference to Thornton's elder brother Fidena, who – with the rest of his family – refuses to acknowledge Thornton and therefore his rank: *see* n. 7 above.

25 *marquis of Rosendale*: John Augustus Sneachie, Jnr., eldest son of the Duke and Duchess of Fidena and godson of Zamorna. (In subsequent Brontë manuscripts 'Rosendale' is spelt 'Rossendale'.)

26 *countess Northangerland*: Lady Zenobia Ellrington, the Verdopolitan Madame de Staël, 'a masculine soul in a feminine casket', a learned woman often referred to as the 'Empress of Women' for her great mental and physical abilities; named after the historical Zenobia, Queen of Palmyra

and the East. Disappointed in her early love for Zamorna, she is now Northangerland's third wife, stepmother to his daughter Mary and therefore, ironically, Zamorna's mother-in-law.

27 *Mr & Miss Montmorency*: Hector Matthias Mirabeau Montmorency (or Montmorenci) is a wealthy Verdopolitan French emigré and sinister influence on Northangerland. Soon after *High Life In Verdopolis*, his daughter Julia elopes with the Angrian artist, Etty (an unacknowledged son of Northangerland), and is later captured by the Ashantees.

28 *lady Somers*: aunt of Zamorna and Lord Charles Wellesley; her name is based on that of a British aristocratic family, one of whose sons fought with Wellington in the Peninsular Wars.

29 *Julia*: Lady Julia Sydney, née Wellesley, favourite cousin of Zamorna.

30 *S' Clair*: Scottish nobleman and friend of the Duke of Wellington; based on the historical St Clairs of Roslin (also Rosslyn), commemorated by Sir Walter Scott in *The Lay of the Last Minstrel*. He is the hero of Charlotte Brontë's story 'The Green Dwarf' (2 September 1833), where his courtship and marriage to Emily Charlesworth are recorded.

31 *haut-ton*: the older French meaning seems to be intended here, referring to the style and manners of the higher echelons of society rather than simply 'high fashion'.

32 *'What's in a name?'*: cf. Shakespeare, *Romeo and Juliet*, II, ii, 43.

33 *princesses Edith & Maria Sneachi*: daughters of Alexander Sneachi (later 'Sneachie'), King of Sneachiesland, and sisters of Fidena and Thornton. Edith, Princess Royal, was betrothed to Lord Frederic Lofty, now presumed dead.

34 *Sir Robert Pelham*: minor politician and landowner from Wellington's Land (or Wellingtonsland); formerly engaged to Mary Henrietta Percy but rejected by her in favour of Zamorna.

35 *Sir John Flower*: formerly Captain John Flower, created Viscount Richton later in 1834 and Verdopolitan Ambassador to Angria. An eminent scholar and Branwell Bronte's pseudonym from 1831 to 1834, he chronicles the rise of the new kingdom of Angria.

36 *lord William Lennox*: young aristocratic coxcomb; named after Lord William Lennox, one of the historical Duke of Wellington's aides-de-camp.

37 *Alexander*: Alexander Sneachi, King of Sneachiesland, one of the four kings of the Glass Town or Verdopolitan Federation.

38 *'the vision for ever, ever vanished'*: cf. Byron, 'Farewell to the Muse', l. 12.

39 *her who went before you*: Marian Hume, Zamorna's second wife, died not only of consumption, but of a broken heart caused by Zamorna's increasing neglect of her: see Christine Alexander, *The Early Writings of Charlotte Brontë* (Oxford: Basil Blackwell, 1983), p. 112.

40 *the basilisk's fascination*: the fabulous king of the serpents, capable of destroying his victims simply by fixing his eyes on them; cf. Spenser, *The Faerie Queene*, IV, vii, 37-9:
> The Basiliske ...
> From powerful eyes close venim doth convay
> Into the lookers hart, and killeth farre away.

41 *'a dirotto pianto'*: in uncontrollable tears; from the Italian: *piangere a dirotto* meaning to cry bitterly, to weep one's heart out.

42 *une femme comme il faut*: a real lady (French): referring to Louisa Vernon, Marchioness Wellesley, former opera singer who married first Lord Dance (or Vernon), then the elderly Edward (also called Richard), Marquis of Wellesley, brother of the Duke of Wellington. Although she is Zamorna's contemporary, her second marriage makes her Zamorna's aunt. She features prominently in Charlotte Brontë's later novelettes as mother of Caroline Vernon and mistress of first Northangerland and then Lord Macara Lofty.

43 *ennuyè*: bored and wearied (French: the feminine form 'ennuyée' should be used here).

44 *if he sees me stand up for a minuet or quadrille, is sure to call for the very quickest & liveliest air he can think of*: the minuet, usually a slow stately dance of French origin, had become faster and more exuberant with Beethoven's music, where it became transformed into a scherzo. The quadrille, a square dance also of French origin, was relatively new in England at this time, having been introduced by the Duke of Devonshire in 1813.

45 *pas*: probably a *pas de deux*, a dance or figure for two people.

46 *Marquis of Marseilles*: Alphonse (or Alexander) Soult, French nobleman who becomes the Angrian Ambassador to Verdopolis and Duke of Dalmatia on the death of his father; named after the historical Marshal Soult, an opponent of Wellington in the Napoleonic wars. Soult is now a respected Verdopolitan poet; formerly Alexander Soult (an early pseudonym of Branwell Brontë) who was mercilessly mocked as Henry Rhymer in Charlotte Brontë's *The Poetaster*.

47 *blue*: nineteenth-century slang for 'blue-stocking', a woman with a taste

for learning: a term traditionally used derisively of a female pedant who neglects 'feminine graces'. The name is derived from a literary society founded by Mrs Montagu about 1750, a prominent male member of which wore blue stockings.

48 *seek for the philosopher's stone or ... perpetual motion*: referring to unattainable goals: according to the alchemists, the philosopher's stone would convert base metals into gold; and perpetual motion is a theoretical force that would move a machine for ever of itself.

49 *General Grenville*: wealthy Verdopolitan mill-owner; based on Lord William Grenville, prime minister of the coalition 'Ministry of all the Talents' (1806) who gave Wellington his first seat in Parliament.

50 *Lily*: Duchess of Fidena, formerly Lily Hart, now wife of Prince John and mother of John Augustus Sneachie, Jnr., Marquis of Rossendale.

51 *cushat*: chiefly Scots and northern dialect: the wood pigeon or ring-dove; cf. Scott, *The Lay of the Last Minstrel*, II, xxxiv.

52 *Abercorn, Eagleton, Molyneux, Lascelles, my cousin Fitzroy*: all extravagant young Verdopolitan noblemen, whose names echo those of British and Irish aristocracy.

53 *Exeunt Omnes*: 'All go out' (Latin), a stage direction for all to retire.

54 *'Yet marked I ... a little azure flower'*: Shakespeare, *A Midsummer Night's Dream*, II, i, 165-6.

55 *petite maîtresse*: woman of affected elegance (French).

56 *overthrew its equilibrium*: Zenobia, now Countess of Northangerland, is renowned for her rages, which were particularly violent after Zamorna, then Marquis of Douro, refused to marry her. In 'Visits in Verreopolis' (7-18 December 1830) and 'The Bridal' (14 July-20 August 1832), Lord Charles Wellesley, whose curiosity makes him a frequent recipient of her rage, presents her as having been driven mad by her jealous love.

57 *Italian fervour & Roman loftiness of which even her soul was capable*: Zenobia is not only a classical scholar with an exceptional mind, but a statuesque woman whose mother was the Castilian beauty, Paulina Louisada. Thus, for Charlotte Brontë, she inherits all the exoticism and passion of the Mediterranean.

58 *on the margins of the costly atlas*: a frequent preoccupation of the young Brontës was sketching in the margins of books or of their own manuscripts.

Several of their own geography volumes are embellished in this way: *see* Christine Alexander and Jane Sellars, *The Art of the Brontës* (Cambridge: Cambridge University Press, 1995), Appendix A.

59 *Two have died from his neglect*: Zamorna's first two wives: Lady Helen Victorine Gordon, who died giving birth to Zamorna's first son Ernest Edward Gordon Wellesley (known as 'Fitzarthur'), and Florence Marian Hume, Marchioness of Douro and mother of Lord Almeda.

60 *Captain Julian Gordon*: early associate of Northangerland and villainous brother of Lady Helen Victorine, Baroness Gordon, first wife of Zamorna.

61 *Arthur O'Connor Esq'*: profligate associate of Northangerland in his youthful days as 'Rogue'; a pugilist and gambler, O'Connor lost his inheritance to Zamorna, who made him head-supervisor of the Angrian Excise.

62 *wrote his name on the oyster shell likewise*: cf. Byron, *Don Juan*, XIV, lxxxi

63 *Lady Percy*: Helen, mother of Northangerland, grandmother and confidante of Mary Henrietta, Duchess of Zamorna, Queen of Angria.

64 *M' Babbicombe Morley*: pompous associate of the Angrian Party; later one of Zamorna's Angrian ministers.

65 *Injustice has deprived him ... nominal)*: *see* n. 7 and 24 above.

66 *the feast of reason & the flow of soul*: Alexander Pope, *The First Satire of the Second Book of Horace Imitated*, l. 127.

67 *Grand Sultan of Turkey surrounded by his Seraglio*: cf. *Jane Eyre*, vol. II, ch. ix: 'I would not exchange this one little English girl for the grand Turk's whole seraglio.'

68 *'the first dark day of nothingness'*: Byron, *The Giaour*, l. 70; for Northangerland's atheism *see* Introduction, p. xii.

69 *Wellington's land*: native country of Zamorna and his family. Although ostensibly African, the geographical features of the four kingdoms of the Glass Town federation are modelled on the British Isles: Parry's Land and Ross's Land are roughly equivalent to Wales and England; Sneaky's Land represents Scotland; and Wellington's Land in the far west is equivalent to Ireland, birthplace of the historical Arthur Wellesley, Duke of Wellington.

70 *Derrinane*: Montmorency's country estate in Wellington's Land, the 'Green Country' (Ireland) of the Glass Town Federation.

71 *Harriette & Frederic*: Lord and Lady Castlereagh; Lady Harriet Castlereagh is Montmorency's eldest daughter.

72 *though Fidena ... should accompany you*: see n. 7 and 24 above.

73 *Allons*: come on, let's go (French).

74 *Bernadotte*: former 'French' associate of Northangerland; later the military leader of Frenchyland who sides with Quashia (the Ashantee leader), Ardrah (Commander of the Verdopolitan navy) and Northangerland against Angria.

75 *A change comes o'er the spirit of our dream*: Byron, 'The Dream': this is the initial line of verses 3-8, previously quoted by Charlotte Brontë in 'Lines on the Celebrated Bewick', 27 November 1832.

76 *la voile du thèatre*: the theatre curtain (the correct French should read 'le voile du thèâtre').

77 *described by Sir John Flower*: in Branwell Brontë's unpublished manuscript 'The Politics of Verdopolis', by Captain John Flower, 23 October 1833 (BPM: B141), where the young Mary Percy is introduced to the Glass Town saga.

78 *welkin*: sky, firmament (chiefly poetical and Lancashire dialect); cf. *Shirley*, vol. III, ch. v.

79 *The Politics of Verdopolis*: see n. 77 above. An interesting deletion occurs here: Charlotte Brontë began writing 'Real Life in' and then substituted 'The Politics of', indicating that she was familiar with the contents of Branwell's latest manuscripts ('Real Life in Verdopolis' and 'The Politics of Verdopolis'). Her own title, 'High Life In Verdopolis', indicates the clear distinction she made in her contrasting role as creator-recorder of the saga.

80 *at the instigation of his own son*: Northangerland's first wife, Augusta di Segovia, arranged the murder of her father-in-law so that her husband (then Alexander Percy) should inherit his money.

81 *the instrument*: namely, Robert Patrick King, or Sdeath (often spelt S'death), ugly associate of Northangerland; a reincarnation of Chief Genius 'Brannii Lightning' (Branwell Brontë, whose first name was Patrick like his father's). Sometime servant and alter ego of the young Northangerland (then 'Rogue'), he is impervious to any attempts to destroy him. His evil relationship with Northangerland (and with his father before him) owes much to James Hogg's study of evil possession and double personality in *Confessions of a Justified Sinner* (1824).

82 *'Justice' we are told 'commends the poisoned chalice &c.'*: Shakespeare, *Macbeth*, I, vii: 'This even-handed justice/ Commends th' ingredience of our poison'd chalice/ To our own lips.'

83 *Roland*: Mary Percy's Newfoundland guard dog, owned by her before her marriage and first described by Branwell Brontë in 'The Politics of Verdopolis' (*see* n. 77 above); he is named after the most famous of Charlemagne's paladins, the flower of French chivalry and subject of romance.

84 *Diana*: Roman goddess of hunting and the woodlands; also goddess of the moon.

85 *Persian Satrap*: governor of a province under the ancient Persian monarchy; Zamorna is increasingly referred to as 'the young satrap of Angria', an image suggestive of his growing tyranny and ostentatious splendour.

86 *Ilderim*: name of the mysterious Saracen in Scott's *The Talisman*. Cf. also Byron, 'To Mr Murray', l. 6; and 'Versicles', l. 5, which refer to Henry Gally Knight's poem *Ilderim. A Syrian Tale*, published by Byron's publisher John Murray in 1816, several years after Byron's own oriental tales appeared. It is possible that Charlotte Brontë read this eastern tale of the robber-hero Ilderim. Knight notes (p. 72) that 'Ilderim, in Turkish, means lightning'.

87 *The light wings of Zephyr ... Gardens of Gul in their bloom?*: Byron, *The Bride of Abydos*, I, i, 7-8.

88 *Zulma*: possibly suggested by Zuleika, heroine of *The Bride of Abydos*.

89 *Suristan*: name possibly suggested by 'Afghanistan'.

90 *Sylla*: 'Scylla' incorrectly spelt here by Charlotte Brontë. In Greek legend, Scylla was a hideous sea monster who was the terror of ships and sailors in the Straits of Messina. Originally a beautiful nymph, she was changed by the jealous Circe into a hideous creature with twelve feet, six heads and a body made up of monsters like dogs which barked unceasingly.

91 *Solomon*: King of Israel, known for his wisdom.

92 *Roland, Roswal, Angria, Calabar, Condor & Sirius.'*: Roswal is Zamorna's favourite stag-hound; Angria and Calabar are named after Angrian provinces; Condor after the huge South American vulture, and Sirius, the Dog-Star; for Roland *see* n. 83 above. Rochester's dog, Pilot, in *Jane Eyre*, was also a Newfoundland dog, probably in imitation of Byron's similar dogs, Boatswain and Lyon. In Italy, according to Shelley, Byron had 'eight enor-

mous dogs' (Elizabeth Longford, *Byron*, London: Weidenfeld and Nicolson, 1976, p. 138). Sir Walter Scott also had a favourite deerhound.

93 *that breed of dogs used at the Cape*: Cape Province, South Africa. Charlotte Brontë may be thinking here of the Cape Hunting dog, but this is a wild, hyena-like dog that hunts in packs.

94 *Moloch … Apollyon*: Moloch was an Ammonite deity worshipped with human sacrifice, usually by fire (Leviticus, xviii, 21, and 2 Kings, xxiii, 10): *see Paradise Lost*, I, 392; II, 43; IV, 357. Apollyon is the Greek name of the king of hell (Revelation, ix, 11), used especially by Bunyan in *The Pilgrim's Progress* (ed. Roger Sharrock, London: Oxford University Press, 1966, pp. 184-8).

95 *cock … blades*: colloquial terms for a gallant fellow. A 'cock' is one who fights with pluck and spirit, like a fighting-cock; a vulgar term of appreciation. A 'blade' is 'a brisk man, either fierce or gay, called so in contempt', Johnson's *Dictionary*.

96 *Rio Grande*: actual river on the west coast of Africa, south of the rivers Senegal and Gambia. Wellingtonsland (or, Wellington's Land) was situated in what is now Senegal, Gambia, Guinea and Sierra Leone; it is renamed in later Angrian manuscripts 'Senegambia'.

97 *Wellington's Glass Town*: capital of Wellingtonsland; the capital cities of all four kingdoms in the Verdopolitan Federation were named after the original Glass Town, now Verdopolis.

98 *The second-sight is on him.*': Warner is a Calvinist; his gift of prescience is usually associated with divine inspiration: a forerunner of Jane Eyre's voice which is also presented as divinely inspired (*Jane Eyre*, vol. III, ch. ix).

99 *I see the lake … wind blowing*: possibly a verse by Charlotte Brontë.

100 *of night & storm & darkness*: cf. Byron, *Childe Harold's Pilgrimage*, III, xcii, 861: a phrase that recurs in several of Charlotte Brontë's stories.

101 *Afrite*: cf. Byron, *The Giaour*, l. 784; and *The Corsair*, II, iv, 150.

102 *settae*: spelling error for 'settee', a long seat or double arm-chair. In this case it is probably a settle, a long wooden bench, usually with arms and a high back, often extending to the ground and having a locker or box under the seat (OED).

103 *Earnest*: spelt 'Ernest' elsewhere in manuscript.

104 *Miss Laury*: Mina, daughter of Ned Laury, a loyal retainer of the Duke

of Wellington. Her early love affair with the youthful Zamorna is nipped in the bud by the Duke, but she becomes Zamorna's mistress after the death of his second wife, Marian, and 'mother' to his children. Probably named after Minna, lover of the pirate Cleveland in Scott's *The Pirate*.

105 *lord Almeda*: Arthur Julius Wellesley, son of Zamorna and his second wife, the late Marian Hume. The title 'Almeida' (as it is spelt elsewhere in early Brontë manuscripts), is derived from the frontier fortress town of Almeida in north-east Portugal, situated on a tributary of the River Douro; during the Peninsular War, Almeida was taken by the French in 1810 but relieved by Wellington the following year.

106 *Fitzarthur*: Ernest Edward Gordon Wellesley, known as 'Fitzarthur' ('Fitz Arthur' or 'Fitz-Arthur') as an indication of his position as a morganatic son of Zamorna by his first wife Lady Helen Victorine, Baroness Gordon, who died in childbirth. The name Gordon originated from Byron's Gordon relatives on his mother's side.

107 *the Calabar*: river in Angria, named after the real river of the same name to the west of the Niger Delta. Calabar is also the name of a town similarly situated in southern Nigeria. Zamorna later establishes Adrianopolis, his new capital of Angria, on its banks.

108 *Bashaw*: arrogant, domineering man; a corruption of the Turkish *pasha*, provincial governor.

109 *'he whistles them* softly *down the wind'*: cf. Shakespeare, *Othello*, III, iii, 266.

110 *like people in a consumption*: the Brontës were especially familiar with the suffering of consumption. Charlotte's two elder sisters had died of the disease, and Emily and Anne Brontë were both to die of consumption.

111 *the broad way of Destruction*: cf. Matthew, vii, 13-14, referred to earlier (*see* n. 5 above).

112 *peine forte et dure*: literally, severe and hard punishment; a French phrase adapted in English to refer to a type of torture (abolished 1772) applied to felons who refused to plead; it usually took the form of pressing the accused between boards until he accepted the trial by jury or died.

113 *De Lisle*: Frederick (or Sir Edward) De Lisle, an eminent Verdopolitan portrait painter, patronised by Zamorna.

114 *Badey Hall*: family residence of Zamorna's second wife, Marian Hume, daughter of Dr Hume Badey.

115 *for some reason she daren't wed him*: Marian was already betrothed to Henry Percy, youngest son of Northangerland, whose death at the hand of his father released Marian to marry Zamorna.

116 *Keswick*: the names Keswick and Grasmere (used below and spelt 'Grassmere' by Charlotte Bronte) are both derived from the Lake District of England, names associated with Wordsworth and Coleridge.

117 *a mavis call*: the call of a song-thrush ('mavis' chiefly Scots dialect, also poetic); frequently mentioned in Scott and Burns.

118 *my hash would have been settled*: 'To settle a person's hash' is to silence or subdue them, to make an end of them (slang).

119 *the deluding portals of ivory or the prophetic gates of horn*: the Gates of Dreams: dreams which delude pass through the Ivory Gate and those which come true pass through the Gate of Horn. A fanciful belief based on two puns in Greek: the words for ivory and 'to cheat with empty hopes' sound the same; and the words for horn and 'to accomplish' also sound the same.

120 *Pale Ghosts & bloodless shapes/ Revisiting the Glimpses of the moon*: cf. Shakespeare, *Hamlet*, I, iv, 53.

121 *The Grass plat*: area of level, grassed ground, usually in front of a house.

122 *mamma's husband ... very near being so at one time*: the occasion is recorded in Charlotte Brontë's story 'Something about Arthur Written by Charles Albert Florian Wellesley', 1 May 1833.

123 *'There are things on earth indeed not dreamt of in our philosophy!*: cf. Shakespeare, *Hamlet*, I, v, 166-7.

124 *Pegasus*: the winged horse, in Greek legend, symbol of poetic imagination.

125 *lord Harry*: the devil, Lucifer, usually used in the mild curse 'By the Lord Harry'.

126 *'in life's morning march when my spirit was young'*: cf. Thomas Campbell, 'The Soldier's Dream', l. 14.

127 *earls Ellrington, or Lofty or Richmond or Harewood, or Sir Markham Howard there, or Bud or Gifford*: contemporaries of the Duke of Wellington: the first four names refer to elderly members of the Verdopolitan aristocracy; the Howards are Angrian gentry; Captain John Bud, a friend of the young Lord Charles Wellesley, is the eminent Glass Town political writer

and pseudonym of Branwell Brontë; John Gifford, a friend of Bud, is a lawyer and antiquarian, probably modelled on William Gifford, first editor of *The Quarterly Review.*

128 *primming*: late seventeenth-century cant: decking oneself out; 'to deck up precisely, to form into an affected nicety' (Dr Johnson).

129 *dominos*: loose cloak, worn chiefly at masquerades, with a small mask covering the upper part of the face (OED).

130 *Red-rover*: pirate ship captained by Northangerland in his youth.

131 *Nereid*: sea-nymph of Greek legend, one of the fifty daughters of Nereus and Doris.

132 *D' Stanhope, wearing ... decorations*: the costumes symbolize the future roles of these characters in the Angrian saga, indicating the forward planning of events by the young authors. Dr Stanhope later wins election as Primate of Angria over his unsuitable rival the Reverend Henry Warner, and Dr Porteus is later appointed Primate of Northangerland Province in Angria.

133 *basquina*: rich outer petticoat, worn by Basque and Spanish women; cf. Byron, *Don Juan*, II, cxx.

134 *Like cardinal Beaufort it made no sign*: *see* Shakespeare, *Henry VI part 2*, III, iii, 29; referring to Henry Beaufort (c.1377-1447), English cardinal and bishop of Winchester, who was responsible for the murder of the Duke of Gloucester.

135 *'He comes! the conquering hero comes!'*: cf. Thomas Morell, *Joshua*, pt iii.

136 *Flower*: *see* n. 77 above.

137 *Maria di Segovia*: also called Augusta di Segovia, part-Italian first wife of Northangerland (then Alexander Percy), on whom she squandered her brother's fortune.

138 *Mary's own mother*: Lady Maria Henrietta Percy, second wife of Alexander Percy and mother of Edward, William, Henry and Mary Percy. Percy was idyllically happy in this marriage but Lady Maria died of consumption, aggravated by the distressful loss of her three sons who were banished from her at birth because of her husband's unnatural aversion to male offspring.

139 *illimitated*: unlimited, unbounded (obsolete).

140 *Good Good!*: possibly an error for the expletive 'Good God!'

141 *'quiet & low, an excellent thing in woman'*: Shakespeare, *King Lear*, V, iii, 272-3.

142 *battle of Velino*: fought during the 'recent' War of Encroachment (December 1833), in which Zamorna won the kingdom of Angria. Angria was officially conferred upon Zamorna by act of parliament in Verdopolis, 9 February 1834, the month before the writing of 'High Life In Verdopolis'.

143 *Robert Sdeath*: *see* n. 81 above; Sdeath's influence here indicates Branwell Brontë's continuing direction of events in the saga. His following ghoulish activity is one of several references in the Brontë juvenilia to body-snatchers, who traded in newly buried corpses to sell them to surgeons for dissection. The practice was widely reported in journals like *Blackwoods*, where Charlotte read about the notorious Burke and Hare case in which victims were smothered so that their bodies could be sold to the Edinburgh surgeon Dr Robert Knox. (Again, Sdeath's Christian name may owe something to this surgeon.)

144 *in accordance to those laws of existence peculiar to our nation, Death had been averted*: reference to the early role of the Chief Genii (the Brontë children) as resuscitators of characters who had been 'killed' in a previous story: *see* Christine Alexander, *The Early Writings of Charlotte Brontë*, p. 34.

145 *poltroon*: coward; from the Italian word for bed (*poltro*), the place preferred by cowards in time of war.

146 *Arundel*: ancient English peerage, with lands in Sussex including Arundel Castle. Thomas Arundel (1353-1414) was Archbishop of Canterbury and Lord Chancellor of England. The names Arundel and Beaufort in this manuscript suggest that Charlotte Brontë was reading a history of the Wars of the Roses at this time, or possibly Shakespeare's history plays, such as *Henry IV* and *Henry VI*.

147 *It is my opinion ... is still bright, fresh & unblown*: the reference here to Zamorna's philandering suggests that Charlotte Brontë had planned a fate for Mary Percy similar to that of Zamorna's two previous wives (*see* n. 59 above); Maria Sneachi, whose role in *High Life* clearly suggests that she is to be instrumental in this plot, is married seven months later to Edward Percy, the disowned eldest son of Northangerland and an industrialist who becomes the Angrian Minister of Trade.

148 *I rather lean to the other opinion*: deliberate obfuscation by Lord Charles Wellesley: Zamorna's son by Soffala, with whom he had an early affair, is the mute dwarf Finic, who is retained as a servant.

TEXTUAL NOTES

The following notes record all additions, deletions, corrections and other significant textual details in the original manuscript pages illustrated in this volume.

Symbols used below:

< >	manuscript deletion
<? >	doubtful manuscript deletion
↑ ↓	added above the line in manuscript
<↑ ↓>	added and subsequently deleted in manuscript
[ ]	editorial insertion

PLATE I:

<Belgium's> ↑Africas↓
artificial<s>
there ↑of↓ artificial in the lives: 'lifes' corrected to 'lives'; 'v' written over 's'
   but 'fe' not deleted in MS.
<is there> among
<st[eep]> narrow
<queen> unlimited
<accelerates> excites
<limbs & bear the man through whose veins flows the clear, or muddy
   current> heart & limbs
an <pass[age]> article: 'n' of 'an' added with 'article'.
<&> which from internal
<was> a dozen
appointments ↑arranged↓ on
these<se> a lady
the ↑coffee &↓ chocolate
<the said> the last
has <fixed upon> met with
<tall or short> very handsome
Young <yes>
<Is not this Wednesd[ay]> I don't doubt
engravings: 'r' written over 'a'
luxurious <luxurious> furniture
<lofty> high
<pocket> handkerchief
about to ↑quit↓ the appartments
<on> at the Entrances
then <what do I>

\<She\> some fragments
this ↑menial↓ office
gardens of \<mosul-patan\> ↑Suristan↓
the \<breathe\> ↑wind↓ to
whispered \<hushed & noiselessly\> ↑still felicity↓
I am ↑just↓ now
\<Mari[a]\> the Princess
\<two\> ↑three↓ months
father ↑shall↓ know
he is ↑she whispered↓ but
duplicate ↑a pair of sententious asses↓ said
sprang: 'g' written over 'r'
wife ↑he↓ drew her
under his ↑own↓
\<What I suppose\> My conduct?
\<two ro[yal]\> ↑a King↓ & princess
\<shine\> sunshine
\<wo[rds]\> tones
sighs is \<in\> incurred
would ↑approve↓ of my
I \<won't\> ↑will not↓ let
\<half the way\> ↑ten miles↓ you
\<?ar[rayed]\> attired
\<& as usual was\> \<↑followed↓\> \<close behind the Duchess of\> my
attention

figures \<two\> ↑too↓ animated
aim \<in view\> in the way
\<?hardened\> ↑decided↓ air
of \<Lord\> ↑little↓ Julius
spring↑ing↓ forward
\<he\> ↑Ernest↓ was
there \<rested\> ↑dwelt↓ on
their \<gleam\> fire
\<arm over\> ↑elbow on↓ the
through ↑the open window amongst↓ laurels
tall ↑young↓ man in black \<who said he\> with

casement ↑& seizing his hand↓ You
Duke ↑silently↓ elevated
if ↑so↓ you
& <two> too
ours <is> ↑are↓ not
with ↑a↓ piercing
<learn> remember
window ↑sill↓ impatient
with a <lovely> cherub flush
gazed ↑fondly yet↓ apprehensively
forehead ↑to↓ which

PLATE 14 (illustration cropped slightly on right):

of the <br[ave]> upright: 'br' not deleted in manuscript
Esquire: 'E' written over 'S'
Altar, Edith: 'E' written over 'N'